Table of Contents

SON'S FAT BLACK FRIEND STOLE MY WIFE & OTHER STORIES OF MILFS GETTING BRED

MILFS BEING BAD COLLECTION 1

PETE ANDREWS

ABOUT THE AUTHOR

I write sexy romances. I used to publish under *xleglover* and *Flash of Stocking* on various sites.

My stories are romances, so they explore the feelings, emotions and relationships of the characters. My stories are also erotica, so the sex scenes are explicit. Often very explicit.

My stories have an emotional edge to them. The characters have thrilling adventures, but there's pain there too, at least for some of them.

I try to write stories that seem like real life. Yes, the situations are extreme, but I hope you come away thinking, *"Yes, I can see how that might happened."*

My wife is my muse, the love of my life. She is the Jennifer in my stories, the Sarahs, the Zoeys. Also also – *gulp* – the Jess's.

You can find my books wherever e-books are sold. If you'd like to join my mailing list or would like to send me a question or feedback, please email me at *peteandrews1701@gmail.com*.

SON'S FAT BLACK FRIEND STOLE MY WIFE

My name is David Smith and my wife is Kristin Smith. We've been married for a little over 20 years. This is the story of how I lost my wife to one of our son's friends, Naeem. Naeem is black, and he's ugly with a brooding forehead, big nose and fat lips, and acne covering his face and back. And he's fat. Seriously fat with a big gut, obese ass, and thick thighs.

I still can't believe I lost my wife to an 18-year-old boy. But what I really can't understand is how I lost her to a fat, ugly, 18-year-old black boy.

My story starts at my son's high school graduation party.

Our house has always been the one where our kids and their friends hangout. My wife and I did it on purpose, because we felt safer having our kids close by. So, when our son Luke graduated from high school, it was only natural that we would throw the party for Luke and his friends. It was a big party. Luke invited practically the entire graduating class.

Our local high school is racially diverse so the high school graduates at the party were mostly white but a good number of black kids, too. My wife and I are white, as are our two kids of course, Luke and his older 19-year-old sister, Mary. Mary wasn't at the party as she was taking a couple of extra classes in college before coming home for the summer.

As always, I was the grill master. Cooking outdoors is my thing and I have an XL Big Green Egg. I wasn't going low-and-slow this evening though. For Luke and his friends, I was going simple with burgers and dogs. The Egg is still good for that though, especially with hamburgers that can soak in some Mesquite smoke. And I had the charcoal in a vortex funnel to limit flare ups.

Around 8pm, the local band we hired for the party got going. It was already dark in our part of the country, so I lit torches around the peripheral of our yard. There were lots of girls at the party in addition to boys, but dancing didn't start right away. We wanted Luke to have a good time, and he's naturally shy, so we needed someone to get the dancing going.

That someone was my wife, Kristin. She's a social butterfly and popular among Luke's friends, so when she dragged one of the boys onto our improvised dance floor, kids quickly joined (including Luke) and soon the dance floor was crowded with dancing bodies.

It wasn't just because Kristin was bubbly and friendly that she was popular among Luke's friends. Kristin is a very attractive woman. She's 42 but looks like a woman in her 30s. Her face is pretty – beautiful when she makes herself up – and framed by dark blonde hair that goes a little past her shoulders.

Even after having 2 kids (one right after the other), Kristin's body is still firm. If anything, the two pregnancies were a benefit because they increased her breast size to 34C (from 34B).

Fitness and health are very important to Kristin, so after both pregnancies she did a lot of hot yoga to get her body back. She still exercises almost every day, although nowadays she's into Pilates.

Kristin has got curves as a woman should, but her tummy is flat, her behind firm, and her thighs tight. In fact, she still has the same thigh gap she had as a teenager, and that's a big source of pride to her.

I was still manning the grill as I watched my wife bopping around on the dance floor with the 18- and 19-year old boys. Kristin was wearing a simple top and skirt and flats – her typical mom outfit – but like always I was proud of the way she looked. Her blouse wasn't tight but it wasn't loose either, and it really showed off her firm breasts. Her skirt kind of flared out at the waist, so even though it was knee length, she was showing off some of her very shapely legs as she danced with the 18- and 19-year-old kids.

I watched as Kristin began dancing with a black boy. I didn't recognize him, but then, I only knew a few of Luke's friends. The young man was tall and even through his loose t-shirt and jeans, it was apparent he was very fit. He was handsome too. From listening to the kids around me at the grill, I learned that the boy's name was Colby and he was the star wide receiver for the school's football team, and he had a scholarship to go to one of the big SEC schools.

At one point, Colby grabbed Kristin's waist and twirled her around, and then he pulled her in close for a quick dip. They circled around each other with their hands touching and their bodies close and even touching at points.

Then, suddenly, Colby grabbed Kristin's waist again. This time, instead of dipping her, he pulled her body against his and he grided against my wife. He did this for long seconds, rubbing his crotch against my wife's.

I couldn't believe what this kid was doing – he was dry humping my wife! And some of the high school grads around me couldn't either. One girl said, "Are you seeing what I'm seeing? Colby is seriously juking with Mrs. Smith!"

I couldn't rush to Kristin's aid. I was still grilling burgers and dogs, and anyway, I knew my 42-year-old wife could handle an 18-year-old kid, even if he *was* a college bound, star football player. I lost sight of Kristin as more kids joined the dance floor. Honestly, I forgot about the incident with Colby as I got busy feeding a big group of high school grads who just arrived to the party.

It was getting late and I went searching for my wife and son. We needed to start winding the party down, and I needed their help to spread the word.

I found Luke on the front porch talking to friends. They were drinking punch from red Solo cups, and I knew immediately from the smell that the punch was spiked with alcohol, probably cheap vodka or rum. Damn! Kristin and I wanted to keep this party alcohol free! After all, these 18- and 19-year-olds were not legal to drink, and many of them were driving home from the party.

Luke wasn't too drunk – just tipsy. He told me I didn't have to worry, because only a few of the kids were drinking spiked punch. He also said it didn't matter anyway, since most people had already left.

I looked over the backyard and realized he was right. From what started as over a hundred party goers, only a couple dozen high school grads were still there. That made me feel better. But as I scanned the remaining crowd, I didn't see my wife Kristin. Luke told me he couldn't remember the last time he saw his mother.

I walked around the yard and didn't see her. I went back into the house through the back door into the kitchen. There was a black kid filling a Solo cup with red punch and vodka. There were big bottles of red punch and Stoli vodka on the kitchen counter. The bottles were mostly empty.

I frowned at the sight. This was not good. How many kids left the party and drove home drunk? And where the hell was Kristin? I was anchored to the grill all night. It was *her* job to make sure kids didn't bring alcohol. Not only did kids bring alcohol, but they brought a lot. Our kitchen looked like a fraternity. Where the hell was my wife?

I searched the house. She was nowhere to be seen.

I finally headed to the basement. I opened the door and saw a black kid there. He said, "Hey, man, nothing going on here."

Then his eyes went wife, like he recognized me. He looked shocked and scared. He immediately bolted up the stairs and took off out of the house.

What the fuck was going on?

I started moving down the stairs when I heard my wife's voice. "Hey, hey, hey," she said. I could tell she was drunk because she was slurring her words. How much of the vodka punch had she drunk?

Kristin said, "Hey, I said stop. I said you could look, not touch."

My eyes went wide with shock. What was going on?

As I slowly crept down the stairs, I heard Kristin giggle and say, "Wait a minute, mister. I'm married and old enough to be your mother. You can't do that."

"You sure don't look like my mamma," a youthful male voice said. I could tell from his voice that he was black. "I'm 18, I'm legal, so don't worry Mrs. Smith, we aren't doing anything wrong."

"You *know* I'm married," Kristin said with that giggle still in her voice. "That makes it wrong."

Then I heard Kristin moan. "Oh god, no don't. God, don't do that ...."

I finally reached the bottom of the stairs. Our basement has a long hallway that leads to a big room with a pool table. We called it, appropriately, the pool table room. There were a couple of storage rooms off the hallway.

I silently crept down the hallway and looked into the pool table room. What I saw shocked me.

Kristin was leaning with her butt against one of the short sides of the pool table. Her blouse was unbuttoned, and her bra pushed up, so her breasts were exposed. At her feet, a black boy was on his knees. It was Colby, the star football player!

Colby was holding Kristin's flared skirt up. He had her panties around her ankles. He was licking Kristin's pussy!

Kristin had her eyes squeezed shut. "Please stop, please, I'm married, please ...."

"I think you like my tongue on your clit, huh, Mrs. Smith?" Colby said. He pushed two fingers into her pussy, and she moaned. The black boy grinned and said, "You like my fingers too, don't you, Mrs. Smith? You're really wet."

"God, please," Kristin begged as Colby moved his mouth back to her sex. "Oh god, oh god …," she moaned as the black boy worked her clit with his tongue.

"Don't listen to the bitch, 88," I heard another male voice say. I could tell he was also black by his voice, although his voice sounded more ghetto than Colby's. "She been teasing us with her MILFy body all night." I couldn't see this second boy, though. He was apparently sitting on the sofa that was on the other side of the wall where I was at.

"More like all my life," Colby said with a big grin at my wife. I saw his teeth were perfect and sparkling white. "I've wanted to get down with you for a long time, Mrs. Smith."

The other black boy laughed. "Tabia gonna kick your ass, 88," the boy said. "She ain't gonna appreciate you wanting to smash this old, white bitch." I figured 88 was Colby's football number. I also guessed Tabia was his girlfriend.

Colby laughed. "Tabia's not around and I can't go two days without getting my dick wet," he said. "Anyway, Mrs. Smith might be old, but look at her, she's smoking hot. And she's prettier than Tabia, but don't tell Tabia I said that, or I'll kick your ass."

The other black boy laughed as Colby went to work on Kristin again. Now he was finger fucking her while also licking her clit.

"Oh god, Colby … Colby, god … I'm cumming Colby … you're making me cum," Kristin moaned with her eyes clenched shut. A moment later, she hugged Colby's head against her pussy and her body shuddered as she came on the black boy's tongue and fingers.

The second boy laughed as he watched Kristin's body shudder from her climax. "You made the bitch cum, 88!" the second boy said. Colby looked back and grinned at his friend as he stood up.

Colby took off his shirt as he stood up. Wow. The black boy was seriously ripped. Combined with his handsome face, I had no doubt he was popular with girls. And, if his football skills were anything close to his looks, he was going to get serious NIL money once in college.

Kristin definitely agreed that Colby had a hot body. She looked at his chest with awe, and said, "God Colby ...."

"You like my body, Mrs. Smith?" Colby asked with a confident laugh as he took both of Kristin's hands and placed them on his chest. It was a testament to how drunk she was – and how attracted she was to the handsome black boy—that she immediately began running her fingertips over Colby's hard pecs and abs. Even though she had just cum, she looked aroused from looking at Colby's handsome face and touching the black boy's ripped chest.

"My turn now, Mrs. Smith," Colby said as he took off his jeans. He wasn't wearing underwear.

I saw his hard cock, and so did Kristin. It looked a little bigger than my penis, which was an average 6 inches.

Colby lifted Kristin onto the pool table. He lifted her easily, that's how strong he was. Kristin's skirt was still up around her waist and now her panties were on the floor.

Colby had a hand on each of Kristin's knees and he opened her legs. He stepped between her legs and took hold of his cock in his hand. He positioned his cock so his head was almost touching Kristin's pussy lips.

"Now you gonna get some black cock, Mrs. Smith," Colby told my wife.

"Colby ...," Kristin said. I thought she was going to tell him again that this was wrong, and he needed to stop. But then my heart sank when she purred, "You're so handsome, Colby. Your body's so amazing. Call me Kristin. Kristin."

Then I felt a dagger through my heart when my wife wrapped her arms around the handsome black boy's neck and kissed him. I could tell she was kissing Colby with her tongue, and knew I was about to see my wife cheat on me for the first time. Was it the first time? Or had she done this before?

You might wonder why I wasn't rushing into the room and demanding that Colby unhand my wife. The truth was, I wasn't able to move. The sight of my beautiful, sexy 42-year-old wife with this 18-year-old, handsome, Adonis-like black boy had me mesmerized. Kristin *was* old enough to be Colby's mother, since he was the same age as our son. And he called her "Mrs. Smith" which further added to the taboo scene taking place in front of my eyes.

I couldn't move. It was like my feet were trapped in concrete. I couldn't move. I was barely able to breathe.

Colby was about to push his dick into my wife when his phone rang. The phone was on the pool table next to Kristin. He looked at it and said, "Fuck! It's Tabia! She's home early and wants to know where I am!"

The second boy laughed as Colby scrambled into his clothes. "Gotta bolt, Mrs. Smith!" he hurriedly said. "You don't wanna see Tabia when she's pissed!"

The second boy was still laughing as Colby turned to go. He said, "Maybe you still get your dick wet with Tabia. She's a slut too, just like this white bitch."

"Fuck you, Naeem, that's *my* slut you're talking about," Colby joked with a grin.

Now I knew the second boy's name. Naeem.

Colby looked at Kristin. She looked confused, like she didn't know what was going on. Her cheeks were flushed and her eyes glazed over. I wondered again how much of that vodka punch she had drunk.

She also looked intensely aroused, and disappointed that the handsome Colby Adonis-god was leaving.

Colby saw the desire in Kristin's beautiful face. He looked at Naeem and laughed. "Hey Naeem, you fat ugly fucker. This is your chance to get some white pussy." With another glance at my wife, he said, "Maybe some other time, Mrs. Smith."

Then Colby bolted up the stairs. I barely had time to step into one of the storage rooms to avoid being seen.

After Colby was gone, I moved back into the hallway, to look back into the pool table room. Kristin was still in the same position. Sitting on the pool table, blouse open and bra pushed up, her skirt around her waist, her legs open. She looked disoriented, like she didn't know where she was, or what she was doing. Her cheeks were still flushed and her eyelids heavy lidded. I'd never seen Kristin so drunk. Or so aroused.

Probably both. Seriously drunk *and* aroused.

Naeem walked over to Kristin, and I saw him for the first time.

Naeem was the complete opposite of Colby. He wasn't handsome. He was ugly with a brooding forehead, big nose and fat lips, and acne covering his face. And he was fat. His gut was so big it fell over the belt of his pants like an apron, jiggling with ever lumbering step he took.

Kristin looked confused as the fat, ugly black boy approached her. A moment ago she had been with Colby, who was handsome and jacked. Now, suddenly, Colby had been replaced by Nareen with his acne-scarred ugly face and fat body. And Nareen's skin wasn't creamy dark like Colby's. Instead, the fat boy's skin was as black as black could be, midnight black.

Nareen was holding a big bottle of vodka and he took a long draw as he approached my wife. He reached a hand to Kristin's bosom and squeezed one of her breasts. He said, "Not bad for an old white bitch."

Then Nareen grabbed Kristin's arm and pulled her off the pool table. "Let's see how good your pretty mouth is," he said as he took another draw of the vodka.

Kristin collapsed to her knees in front of Nareen. "Here, slut, drink up," Nareen said, handing the vodka bottle to Kristin. Kristin took a big gulp, and then she had to put a hand to the floor to keep from falling over. I had never seen my wife so wasted. Probably, Nareen wanted to keep her drunk so she would do whatever he wanted.

"Come on, bitch, you know what to do," Nareen said impatiently. Kristin gathered herself and rose up onto her knees. She unbuckled his belt and then tugged at his loose jeans. When they wouldn't come down, she focused on one side at a time. She pulled one side then the other, going back and forth an inch at a time, until she managed to get them below his knees. The fat black slob took another pull from the vodka and said impatiently, "Get on it bitch, I ain't got all day."

I was shocked Kristin was being so submissive, and obedient. Maybe for Colby, but for this ugly, fat brute?

Again, you might wonder why I wasn't rushing into the room and tearing my wife away from Naeem. The truth was, I still wasn't able to move. I was fascinated to see what would happen, like not being able to take my eyes off a train wreck. A moment ago, it had been Kristin with the Adonis-like Colby. Now, it was my beautiful, sexy wife with this fat, ugly black boy. I was mesmerized by this train wreck happening just 15 feet in front of me. My feet were trapped in concrete. I couldn't move. I could barely breathe. My heart was pounding.

With her right hand, Kristin lifted his belly to get access to cock. Her eyes got big when she saw it for the first time. I was shocked too. Naeem's cock was huge, easily twice as long as mine and much thicker. *Fuck!* Unlike Colby, Naeem had a Big Black Cock.

Still supporting Naeem's fat belly with her right hand, Kristin wrapped her left hand around his shaft. He was so thick her fingertips didn't touch. I felt a stab in my heart as I saw the diamonds of her wedding and engagement rings sparkle while her hand was around Naeem's black cock.

Kristin tentatively moved her head forward. With open lips, she took the black boy's cock into her mouth.

God, I couldn't believe what I was seeing! My wife had another man's penis in her mouth!

Kristin couldn't take much of Naeem's fat, long cock into her mouth. So instead, she licked down the shaft, and then licked his balls. Naeem moaned and said, "That's it bitch, you doing okay, keep doing that."

My insides turned over as I watched Kristin – my wife – turn into a frenzied slut as she licked the young black boy's cock and balls. She worshipped his cock not only with her mouth but with her breasts and fingers.

And Kristin moaned as she played with Naeem's BBC. She was getting off on this! It was like she was obsessed, moaning and purring as she licked and fondled the fat cockhead, thick shaft, and big balls.

But Naeem was done with Kristin's teasing. He took his hard cock into his hand and rammed it into Kristin's mouth. "Blow me bitch!" he growled.

Kristin swallowed a few inches of Naeem's manhood – that was all she could take without gagging – and then sucked him as she feverishly pumped the 8 or 9 inches of cock meat that she couldn't stuff into her mouth. I'd never seen her so carried away. Kristin, lost in total abandon, along with the contrast between her fair white skin and his jet-black skin, along with their difference in looks (Kristin being beautiful and slim, Naeem being ugly and fat), made for the most erotic thing I had ever seen in my life. It was actually better than if it had been my wife with the Adonis-like Colby.

"Ah, yeah, that's it. Get it bitch. Get my cock good. You done this before. You love black cock. Tell me bitch ... tell me what you thinking about my cock."

Kristin took Naeem's cock out of her mouth but she continued to stroke him with her two hands. "I can't help it," she said, looking helpless but aroused beyond belief. "This is so wrong. I'm married. I'm cheating on my husband. But I can't help it."

"Yeah, you a cheating bitch," Naeem said with a big triumphant grin on his fat, acne-scarred face. He pulled Kristin to her feet and pushed her against the pool table. He wasn't nearly as strong as Colby, so he needed Kristin's help to raise her ass onto the edge of the table.

Now, Kristin was back where she had been moments ago (although then with Colby), sitting on the pool table, blouse open and bra pushed up. Naeem pushed her skirt up until it was around her waist. He roughly jerked her legs open and stepped between them.

"Now you gonna get fucked," Naeem said. He lifted his gut, exposing his hard cock. I saw the fat cockhead was pressing against Kristin's pussy lips.

"Please wear a condom!" Kristin begged. "I'm not on the pill!"

My head exploded as I remembered. We weren't *trying* to have another child, but we weren't *not* trying either. Kristin was 42, so we were talking about whether we wanted another child before she got too old. We couldn't decide, so Kristin had gone off the pill. We would let God make the choice for us. She went off the pill a few months ago, so any lingering useful effects of the pill were gone. My wife was completely unprotected.

And now this ugly, fat black kid was going to fuck her bareback. Now he – instead of God, instead of me, her husband – was going to make the decision for us.

Other than lifting his fat belly and pulling my wife closer to him, there was no other foreplay. Naeem guided his cock with his hand, and then he pushed forward.

I gasped! Another man's cock was inside my wife! A black cock was inside my wife!

Kristin cried out when his cock penetrated her pussy. "Go slow, go slow!" she begged, pressing her palms against his jiggling, fat man boobs to stop him from thrusting more inside her.

"I know how to fuck, bitch," Naeem said derisively. He pushed his cock into Kristin slowly. He was grimacing and beads of sweat gathered on his forehead, like he was exerting himself to penetrate my wife fully. "Fuck you got a tight cunt, bitch," he said.

After Naeem was about halfway inside Kristin's pussy, he began to pull out and push back in. With each inward thrust, he pushed more of his thick shaft into her.

"Oh god, oh god, it's so big!" Kristin cried. Her eyes were tearing up, she was in pain. "It feels like you're tearing me open!"

Naeem ignored her and kept slowly fucking her. With each thrust forward he penetrated her pussy with a little more of his thick shaft.

"Oh god it's too much!" Kristin cried. Her eyes were clenched shut and her face was full of anguish. The black boy was really hurting her. I was about to go to her rescue when she moaned, "It feels so good! I love it! Don't stop! Please don't stop!"

I felt like a bus had run me over. My wife *wanted* to be fucked by this fat, ugly black boy!

"I ain't stopping, bitch," Naeem said as he began to quicken his pace. He began fucking Kristen harder, and faster.

Kristin was moaning and grunting continuously. I had never heard these sounds from her! Then her body spasmed and jerked, her toes curled, and she cried out as she came hard on Naeem's big black cock.

Naeem didn't seem to notice Kristin's orgasm on his cock. He was thinking about himself. His face was a mix of concentration and pleasure. "Fuck, your white pussy feel good! It tight and milk my cock! Gonna nut in you, bitch! Here cums! Gonna nut you!"

I was hoping Kristin would beg Naeem to pull out. But she did the opposite. She wrapped her arms and legs around the black boy (the best she could, since he was so fat), encouraging him to push even deeper into her womb.

Naeem roared when his orgasm hit. He put his pudgy hands on my wife's shapely hips and held her tight as he rammed his entire cock into her pussy. With his cock lodged as far as it would go inside Kristin's body, he orgasmed and ejaculated his virile black seed into her unprotected womb.

Naeem collapsed onto Kristin after his orgasm ended. He was gasping. With his obese body on top of her, I could barely see my wife, and I was worried she wouldn't be able to breathe. Apparently though,

Naeem must have been supporting at least some of his weight on his arms.

Then Kristin did something that I couldn't believe, and that broke my heart. She wrapped her arms around Naeem's neck and pulled his face to hers. Then she tenderly kissed the fat lips of this ugly boy with the acne-scarred face.

I couldn't take anymore. I ran up the stairs into the kitchen. I needed to out of the house, I needed to get away. I grabbed the car keys and drove away.

I drove for a a long time, aimlessly. My head spun. It was impossible to process what I had just seen.

My wife of 20 years had just cheated on me! With a black boy! A fat, ugly black boy!

———●———

I FINALLY DROVE BACK home. Our yard and house were dark. The party was long over.

I walked into my house. I walked up the stairs. I walked into the bedroom I shared with Kristin. I wasn't sure what I would see. I was afraid of what I might see.

But there she was, my wife, looking completely normal. Kristin was awake. Clearly she'd been waiting for me.

Kristin bolted up from the bed and ran to me. She hugged me as she cried, "Oh god, David, where were you? I was so worried!"

I could tell Kristin had showered. Her dark blonde hair still felt damp. And I smelled the familiar scent of the shampoo she always used. Strawberry vanilla.

I pushed Kristin away and held her at arm's length. I opened her robe and saw she wore what she always wore to bed. An XL jersey of her favorite football player (Patrick Mahomes)— the jersey draped over her slim, petite body – and little white cotton socks on her feet. The white socks were dotted with little red Elmo's, because she had always loved the Sesame Street character.

I looked at her in the Mahomes jersey and the Elmo socks. She looked completely normal. She looked like my wife.

"What?" Kristin asked as my eyes roamed over her face and body.

Then I abruptly pushed Kristin onto the bed. I tore off the jersey.

"David, what?" Kristin yelped.

I looked at my wife's body. She was naked except for panties and the Elmo socks. Her body looked the same. Her breasts looked the same.

Then, again without warning, I ripped the panties from her hips. Again Kristin yelped.

I tore off my clothes. Then I rammed my hard cock into her. I fucked her hard and fast, not caring about whether she was getting any pleasure out of it. When I was about to cum, I grabbed her hips as I'd seen Naeem do a few hours before. I pumped my sperm into my wife's unprotected womb.

Just as I'd seen Naeem do a few hours before.

After I was done, I collapsed onto my back, next to Kristin. She squealed, "David, what was that?"

I was still panting when I said, "I saw that black boy fuck you."

Then Kristin was crying, trying to hug me, trying to kiss me, begging me to forgive her. As she sobbed, the story came out.

It took hours, and half the time I couldn't understand what she was saying because she was crying so hard. But finally as the sun was rising, I understood what had happened.

No, that's not accurate.

I understood *why* it had happened.

———◦———

KRISTIN'S FATHER WAS a red-neck bigot. She grew up with him always making demeaning jokes about "niggers" chasing after white girls (yes, her father still to this day regularly used the N-word). He said over and over:

Blacks targeted white girls, wanting to steal them from their white boyfriends.

Blacks lived to prove that white boys with their little white boy dicks couldn't fuck like black boys.

Blacks especially chased after blonde girls –niggers wanted to bred blonde girls to make blonde hair and blue eyes extinct.

Blacks wanted to ruin white girls. They wanted white girls to get addicted to their big cocks. They wanted to ruin white girls by getting them pregnant with their nigger babies and make their pussies loose so they became worthless to white boys and their little white boy dicks.

⸻●⸻

ALL THROUGH HIGH SCHOOL, whenever Kristin told her parents she was going on a date, her father would always warn, "He better not be a nigger."

Kristin told me she *did* date a black boy once. I was surprised by that. I knew her father was a bigot, and while she was not prejudiced, I always assumed some of his biases had rubbed off on her. What do they call it? Implicit bias?

She shook her head as I said this. "I don't know," she said. "I guess that's mostly true. But also, it kind of became a fantasy for me. Hearing my father say, 'black boys want to ruin white girls'—I don't know, it sounded so evil, it kind of became a fantasy for me."

"Why haven't you ever told me this fantasy?" I asked.

"*How* could I tell you this fantasy?" Kristin said. "Have you told me all *your* fantasies?"

It was true. I had not told her all my fantasies.

Kristin's best friend has a daughter, Callie. Her face is average, but she has the firmest breasts, the sexiest stomach, the longest legs. Below the neck she was every man's wet dream, and the fact her face was (at best) plain somehow just made her more sexy. I have imagined myself in bed with Callie. Many times. Obviously, this was a fantasy I could not tell my wife.

"Tell me about this black guy you dated," I said, sidestepping any discussion of my fantasies.

The boy's name was Jaxon. He was tall and handsome, with broad shoulders and muscular legs. As Kristin described Jaxon, it sounded like she was talking about Colby.

Jaxon got Kristin into her bed on their first date. Which shocked me, because it had taken three dates before she even let me kiss her much less get into her pants.

I thought I knew Kristin's sexual history. We were like all couples. Over time we talked about our past relationships, our past loves, our past lovers. Up to that moment, I had thought my wife had slept with 5 guys before me. Now I knew it was 6.

"Was Jaxon's cock as big as Naeem's?" I asked.

"About as big," Kristin whispered. She was being cautious, afraid I was going to kick her out of the house and ask for a divorce.

"Did you cum as hard with Jaxon as you came with Naeem?" I asked.

Kristin shrugged. She didn't want to answer. But I could tell by her face and her body movements that she had.

"So, why didn't you marry Jaxon?" I asked.

Kristin's eyes jerked wide with shock. She said, "David, god, I could never marry a black man!"

I stared at my wife. *Now* she sounded like her father. But at least I understood why her relationship with Jaxon never went beyond physical.

But I still didn't understand. Why Naeem? Sure, he was black, and he had a big cock. But he was vile, with an ugly face and a fat body. How could she let this fat, ugly black boy touch her much less suck his dick and put his cock into her?

When I asked, she meekly said, "I was drunk—." I cut her off.

"Don't lie, Kristin," I said angrily. "Yes, you were drunk, and if you ended up fucking Colby, that I'd understand. It would've been like, re-living your fling with Jaxon. That I could understand. But Naeem? Fat, ugly Naeem?"

"I don't know," Kristin said with a helpless look, and it was clear she was being honest. She *didn't* know. "It's just, Colby got me so hot. And then, yeah, Naeem is fat and ugly. But somehow, that made him even more hot. Or like, not him, but the scene was hotter. Especially when I saw how big he was."

I stared at Kristin. I understood what she was talking about. The fact Callie had an ugly face to go along with her hot body made my fantasy of fucking her even hotter.

As I was thinking this, Kristin was still talking. It was almost like she was talking to herself, trying to come to grips with what had happened.

She hesitantly said, "I don't know ... the way my father talked about white girls and black boys—it was like white girls were submissive to black boys. And you know how I am, about submissiveness. The way Naeem treated me, the way he called me bitch and cunt ... it turned me on."

I stared at my wife again, trying to process all this. We finally fell asleep, not waking until noon. I took the day off.

As soon as I woke up, I fucked Kristin again. It wasn't making love. It was fucking.

Then we went to the drug store to get a morning after pill. If she was pregnant, there was a chance the baby was mine. But more likely it was Naeem's, since he was younger and his sperm more virile (probably). Anyway, I wasn't going to take a chance that a black baby was going to pop out of my wife's stomach.

Kristin made my favorite dinner, chicken and dumplings, the dish my mother always made for my birthday. As she worked at the stove, I pressed my body against her and fucked her again.

Then before bed, I fucked her again. Finally, we both fell asleep, emotionally and physically exhausted.

The next day after work, Kristin met me at the door, her hair and makeup perfect, wearing my favorite outfit, a tight-fitting dress with stockings and high heels. She had my favorite cocktail in her hand, and on the table was my favorite red wine and the chicken and dumplings (we never got to it last night).

Before dinner, I bent Kristin over the sofa and fucked her. Then after dinner, I fucked her again on the pool table, just like Naeem had.

As we panted with me on top of her, Kristin asked, "What's going on, David?"

She meant of course, what was going on with me wanting sex with her so much? Normally, we had sex maybe once a week. Sometimes we didn't have sex for a few weeks. Now since her hookup with Naeem, we'd have sex – how many times? I'd lost count.

I wanted to believe I just wanted to reclaim my wife. But I knew it was more than that. I couldn't deny it. Seeing my beautiful, sexy wife with the ugly, fat Naeem turned to on!

I said, "If you had a choice, would you fuck Colby or Naeem tomorrow?"

I knew she could have either black boy. She was a sexy MILF after all. All it would take was one phone call.

"David, I don't—," Kristin began to protest, but I cut her off.

"Which one?!!!!" I hissed.

Kristin hesitated for long moments. Then she meekly said, "Naeem."

Her admission drove me wild with rage. And lust! Suddenly I was hard again! I pulled Kristin off the pool table, onto her knees just as

Naeem had done! I rammed by hard cock into her mouth! I fucked her face, chanting, "Take it! Take it! Take it!"

———————•———————

ABOUT A WEEK LATER, Kristin had her eyes downcast when she said, "Naeem texted me."

I took her phone and looked at the text. It was a picture of his big black cock and the message was, "Gonna nut in you again slut."

"He gets right to the point, doesn't he?" I joked with a laugh. My laugh was anything but jovial.

"Yeah," Kristin said. She looked bothered.

"Why are you showing me this?" I said, anger and excitement in my voice. "Why didn't you just delete his text?"

"I don't know," Kristin said, her voice so low it was practically a whisper. "I thought you might want to see it."

My cock was rock hard in my pants. I texted back to Naeem (pretending to be Kristin), "Come to my house tomorrow."

Kristin looked incredulous at me, like she didn't believe what I'd just done.

A moment later, Naeem texted back "You look good for me bitch."

I jumped on Kristin and fucked my wife hard. Afterwards, while we were both panting, I told her, "You're gonna dress really sexy tomorrow, to look good for that fat, ugly black boy." Kristin moaned at my words.

Then I added, "And don't wear panties. I don't want anything between your cheating pussy and his big black cock."

———————•———————

THE NEXT DAY I TOOK off from work. I wanted to watch Kristin with Naeem again.

At the party, Kristin had worn one of her typical mom outfits, a simple top and skirt and flats. Tonight, though, she had to dress up to look good for Naeem.

First Kristin did her hair and makeup so she looked like a sexy movie star. Then she dressed in a body-hugging dress that swooped in the front and ended well short of her knees. She wore a bra because she was insecure about the slight sag in her big tits, even though at 42-years-old her tits were still magnificent. She wore black thigh high stockings and 4-inch high heels.

As I told her, she didn't wear panties.

My wife looked as good and desirable as I had ever seen her.

It was late when Naeem arrived. The house was dark so I could watch from the shadows. Kristin stood in front of Naeem as he looked at her. "You look good for an old bitch," he said. He grinned as he said this. I saw the ugly black kid had uneven, yellow stained teeth. His teeth were as ugly as the rest of his fat body.

"What yo name?" Naeem asked. "Colby say you Smith?"

"That's my last name," my wife said. "My name is Kristin. Kristin Smith."

Naeem slowly nodded, his eyes still on my wife's body. "Sit Kristin," Naeem said, motioning to the sofa in our living room.

Kristin sat and Naeem got on his knees in front of her. He pushed up the skirt of her dress and paused when he saw the lacy tops of her thigh high stockings. He rubbed his thumb over the lace. With a grin that showed off his stained teeth again, he said, "White boys like this shit, right?"

Kristin shuddered at his words. Naeem's words excited her because they reminded her of what her father had said many times – "niggers want to steal pretty white girls from their white boyfriends."

Naeem pushed Kristin's skirt up until it was around her waist. He nodded approvingly when he saw she wasn't wearing panties. He spread her legs and said, "I wanna taste your white cunt." Then Naeem folded his body over his fat gut and began eating my wife out.

This surprised me. I figured Naeem would want oral sex from Kristin. I didn't think he would be giving anything.

Clearly Kristin assumed the same thing, because there was surprise all over her beautiful face. But then her face turned serious, and her cheeks got flushed as Naeem's tongue kept working on her. I saw Kristin grip the cushions of the sofa and the muscles of her firm thighs tense as Naeem licked between her pussy lips and over her clitoris.

Naeem raised his head for a moment. "You like this cunt," he said with a grin. It wasn't a question, it was a statement. He could tell he was getting to her, probably by how her body was responding and how wet she was getting.

Naeem pushed two of his fat fingers into Kristin's pussy, and she groaned, "Ugh, god ...."

Naeem began finger fucking her, at the same time lowering his head again and swirling his tongue over her clit. Moments later, Kristin grabbed the back of Naeem's head, curling her manicured fingers in the black boy's dirty, unruly afro, and her body jerked and she moaned as she had her first orgasm of the night.

The black boy didn't give Kristin time to recover from her orgasm. He stood up and pulled her to her high heeled feet. "We gonna fuck proper this time," he said as he marched my wife up the stairs.

Kristin steered Naeem to our guest bedroom. He shook his head no. "This ain't where your little dick white hubby fuck you," he said when he saw the small full-size bed. He pulled Kristin to our master bedroom across the hallway.

"No, please, not here!" Kristin begged. "Not my husband's bed!"

Naeem laughed dismissively. That was *exactly* what he wanted, to fuck Kristin in her *husband's* bed.

"Doggy, slut," Naeem ordered as he pushed Kristin onto the bed. My wife obediently got on her hands and knees.

Naeem got on the bed behind Kristin. Our bed creaked and sagged so much from the weight of his obese body that I thought it might split in two.

Naeem pushed up Kristin's skirt again, exposing her bare ass and stockinged legs. He slapped her ass hard, once, twice, three times. She yelped in pain, but arousal was painted across her beautiful MILF face. I had never treated Kristin this way. Was it possible this abuse turned her on?

Naeem pulled down his pants. Again his fat belly sagged so much, his cock was hidden. But now both me and Kristin knew what he was packing.

Naeem used one had to lift his fat stomach, and used the other hand to guide his cock to Kristin's married pussy. He pushed forward and penetrated my wife.

"Ugh, god! So big!" Kristin groaned. It was just like last time. It was painful at first, but I knew the pain would soon turn to pleasure.

And that's what happened. After a few minutes of Naeem moving his big cock in and out of her, Kristin was moaning and groaning just like last time, her manicured fingers clutching the sheets as her orgasm built and built.

Then suddenly, Kristin cried out and her body spasmed violently as her orgasm hit. It was a huge orgasm, like a tidal wave crashing down on the beach. She collapsed onto her chest and babbled incoherently as she tried to the process the intense pleasure this black boy had just given her.

Naeem wasn't going to give her time to recover, though. He reached under and pulled her back to her hands and knees. As he began fucking Kristin again, he unzipped her dress and pulled it down her shoulders, then he unsnapped her bra.

Naeem roughly groped Kristin's big, magnificent breasts as he fucked her hard. "Good tits for an old bitch, but saggy too," he said. Kristin moaned at his demeaning words, as they pushed her submissive and humiliation buttons.

"Your pussy tight for an old bitch," Naeem said as he was nearing his orgasm. "Cause your white boy hubby got a little white boy pencil dick."

Kristin moaned again. Naeem's demeaning words about white boys – *about her husband!* – reminded her of what her father had said for years, and played into her black over white domination fantasies.

Despite the intense lust she was feeling, there was still some good sense in at least a corner of Kristin's pretty head. She said pleadingly, "Please pull out Naeem! I'm not on birth control!"

"Too bad bitch," Naeem said uncaringly. "Gonna nut your pussy. If you get fat with my black baby, too bad for you. Too bad for little dick hubby."

And then Naeem was cumming. He gripped Kristin's hips tight so she couldn't pull away. He wanted to be so deep inside her pussy, none of his sperm would leak out.

Feeling the powerful jets of Naeem's black seed splashing against her walls pushed Kristin over the edge again. Especially when she remembered her father's words, "niggers want to bred blonde girls to make blonde hair and blue eyes extinct."

Kristin's sexy MILF body shuddered for long moments as the tendrils of her orgasm flittered through her firm sexy body. Naeem kept his cock inside her pussy, wanting to plug his black sperm inside her.

Eventually Naeem pulled his cock out. Even though it was softening, his big black cock still looked like a dangerous black python. "Where hubby sleep?" the black boy asked.

"What?" Kristin said, not understanding. Her head was still swirling from all the intense orgasms the black boy had just given her. "There. On the right."

Naeem grinned, showing his uneven yellow teeth again, and then he used my pillow to clean his filthy cock. "Fuck your husband later on that," he said with a demeaning laugh.

Naeem got off the bed. Again our bed creaked with his movements, and I was certain we'd need a new bed soon if Kristin continued to fuck this boy.

Naeem got dressed and then he moved back to the bed. He reached behind Kristin's head and pulled her face to his. "Kiss me bitch," the black boy said, and then he was open mouth kissing my wife's mouth.

I felt sorry for Kristin, having to kiss this fat, ugly black boy with his stained teeth. Given how his teeth looked, his breath was probably foul. And the fact she was pressing her beautiful smooth face against his ugly, acne scarred face was disturbing. But she didn't resist his kisses. They sucked face for long moments, and I could tell they were tonguing each other.

After Naeem finally pulled away, he grabbed Kristin's breasts. "Your sagging tits are mine now," he said. Kristin nodded.

"And your pussy too," Naeem said as he cupped Kristin's pussy with his fat black hand. Kristin nodded again.

"Say it bitch," Naeem ordered.

"My breasts and pussy belong to you now," Kristin said obediently.

"Not you husband. Me," Naeem said.

"Not my husband," Kristin said submissively. "My breasts and pussy belong to you."

The fat black boy smiled. He grabbed her breasts again and said, "Your saggy old tits ain't so bad." My eyes got big at his words. I was surprised. So was Kristin. Naeem had actually said something nice to my wife. It was practically a tender moment.

⸺⬤⸺

AFTER NAEEM WAS GONE, I emerged from the bathroom, which had doors from both the hallway and our master bedroom. I'd been watching and listening to everything through a crack in the door.

Kristin was still in the position Naeem had left her in. Her dress around her waist like a wide belt. Her breasts exposed with her bra hanging from one strap on her right arm. Her thigh high stockings laddered from mid-thigh to past her knees. Somehow, the sexy stiletto high heels were still on her smooth, pretty feet.

My cock was steel inside my pants. I got on the bed with Kristin, and noticed it didn't have the same firmness as before. Naeem was definitely ruining my bed, just like he was ruining my wife's tight pussy.

Suddenly I was angry, and I threw Kristin down on her hands and knees. I was going to treat her like a worthless dog, just as Naeem treated her.

I pushed my cock into her pussy. Fuck she was so loose! And slick with Naeem's sperm inside her!

I pressed her face into my pillow that Naeem had soiled with his cock. "Slut! Slut! Slut!" I growled as I fucked my slutty, cheating wife with everything I had.

I didn't last long. No way I could last long after what I had witnessed. Within moments I came and added my spunk to Naeem's.

I pulled out of Kristin and fell onto my back. Gasping, I said, "He came inside you again. We need to go to the drugstore tomorrow."

———◦———

THE NEXT DAY AT THE drugstore, Kristin and I got another Plan B pill from the pharmacy. The pharmacist was the same one as last week, and he looked questioningly at us as we asked for another morning after pill. But he didn't ask the question on his lips.

I was tempted to tell the pharmacist, *"Yeah, shit head, that's right, my wife is fucking an ugly fat black kid because he's got a big cock and he fucks her better than me. But I don't want a fucking black baby so that's why we need the Plan B."*

We bought a bottle of water so Kristin could take the morning after pill. I needed some air so I told her I would meet her at the car.

What I didn't know was, Kristin looked at the pill for long moments. She touched her flat stomach as she remembered what her father said, "Nigger boys want to bred blonde girls because they want to make blonde hair and blue eyes extinct." She shivered at the memory. Kristin looked at the pill for a moment longer. Finally, reluctantly, she put the pill in her mouth and washed it down with water.

⁌ ◆ ⁍

OUR SON LUKE WAS A lifeguard at the local pool, and when he was off, he hung with his friends. Since they had graduated and would go to college soon, they wanted to spend as much time together that they could.

And our daughter Mary decided to take a summer school class, so she was away at college for the summer.

That gave Kristin and me a lot of privacy, and we needed it. After getting home from the drugstore, Kristin sat next to me and said, "How do you feel, David?"

"Not great," I admitted. I was still bothered from last night. With sarcasm in my voice, I said, "I guess no husband likes to learn his wife's breasts and pussy belong to someone else."

Kristin looked down at her feet, ashamed. With a soft voice, she said, "You know I said that just in the moment."

I angrily hissed, "You loved getting fucked again by Naeem! I still can't believe you're attracted to that fat ugly kid!"

"I explained it to you. I'm not attracted to *him*," Kristin insisted, still talking in that soft voice. "It's just, it makes it so wrong and wicked – you know, my father hating black people, and making them all taboo to me – I think that is what gets me so hot."

I shrugged and said, "I guess."

Then she looked into my eyes and said with a gentle voice, "I don't think we can just talk about me. There's you too."

"What do you mean?"

"David, I can't remember the last time we've had so much sex," Kristin said. "And it was *you* pretending to be *me* and asking Naeem to come over."

Now it was me looking down at my feet. Because what she said was true. But I didn't say anything. I couldn't admit to her – to myself – that it turned me on to see my wife with another man. No, not a man. A kid. A black boy. And yes, like Kristin, the fact Naeem was fat and ugly added to the turn on.

Finally, I said, "I think you should go back on the pill."

Kristin stared at me. She knew the implications of that. Go back on the pill. So she could keep fucking Naeem. Without getting pregnant with his black baby.

"Okay," Kristin said after a moment's hesitation, her eyes downcast again.

She didn't say, *"This is crazy, it's risky, we should stop."*

Instead she simply said, "Okay."

Then I saw something in her beautiful face. Remembering what her father had said many times, I said, "Unless you *want* that nigger to bred you and put a nigger baby in your belly."

It was the first time in my life I had said the N word. And now I just said it twice in one sentence.

But it had the effect I suspected it would. Kristin's cheeks flushed red and she immediately looked aroused. She leaned her sexy body into me and said, "Make love to me, David."

Then we were kissing. And undressing. And making love.

<hr>

KRISTIN DIDN'T GO BACK on the pill. And she kept fucking Naeem. Once a week, sometimes twice. The night before we took our son Luke to college, she was in our bed – in *my* bed – with Naeem wearing stockings and high heels, and getting her brains fucked out by the fat, ugly black boy.

Somehow, Kristin hadn't gotten pregnant, even though Naeem never used a condom. He never pulled out. He always came – or what he called it, he *nutted* – inside my wife. We began thinking that maybe at 42, she was too old to get pregnant again.

———◉———

THEN CAME THE EVENING that everything got crazy. Really crazy. Insane.

Usually Naeem came to our house to fuck Kristin. I had stopped watching. There was only so much a man can take. I should have put my foot down to stop this madness, but I could tell Kristin was still into it. Or should I say, she was into Naeem being into her.

I figured we were empty nesters now with both Luke and Mary at college. We were still relatively young, Kristin 42 and me 45. Maybe this was the time in our lives to do crazy things. We'd then have these memories to fuel our sexy pillow talk for the rest of our lives.

Also, I was still thinking about Callie, the daughter of my wife's best friend. With her tight, ripe teenager body and plain, borderline ugly face ....

Callie wasn't legal yet, but she would be turning 18 eventually. Could I somehow seduce Callie into my bed? Maybe, if Kristin helped me.

And maybe Callie at that point would still be a virgin. Even though she had a fantastic body, boys her age might not be interested because of her face.

If I got to pop a virgin teenager's cherry? On top of Callie being the daughter of my wife's best friend? On top of the allure of fucking a girl who was amazing from the deck down, but who should wear a bag over her head? It frankly made me dizzy thinking about it. And it wasn't like Kristin could object. Letting Naeem into her pussy for months now, she didn't have any moral ground to stand on. She got her turn. Now, not only would she have to let me do anything I wanted with the daughter of her best friend, she would probably feel obligated to help me get into the teenager's skin-tight skinny jeans.

On this evening, Naeem said he wanted to take Kristin out. He was kinda getting attached to my wife. Like a crush. Anyway, he said he wanted to show Kristin his house and how he lived. Let her get to know him better.

Kristin thought Naeem was being sweet. She promised to be home by midnight. I didn't care she was going to his place. This would make it easier for me, as I wouldn't have to leave the house – *my* house – while Naeem fucked her in my bed. Like I said, I had stopped watching from the shadows. I typically went to the movies or dinner someplace during their hookups.

So, I wasn't there when all this happened. I put this together from what Kristin told me. And what I forced out of Colby. You remember, the handsome, Adonis-like star wide receiver? Yes, he saw it all too.

Kristin drove to the address Naeem gave her. It was his house, a dilapidated, run-down shack in the poorest part of town. Naeem's parents weren't there, because they worked Saturdays, and they worked long shifts. The house was empty and would be until the morning.

Naeem gave Kristin vodka punch, like he had at the graduation party. Once she was drunk, he gave her a pill. He told her it would make sex better. I'm pretty sure it was Molly – Ecstasy. Anyway, Naeem was able to talk Kristin to take it because she was already drunk.

Naeem got Kristin into his bed – she wasn't objecting, that was why she was there, to fuck. And they did fuck, with Kristin naked except for her thigh high stocks and 4-inch stiletto high heels.

Naeem fucked Kristin bareback like he always did, and when she came her orgasm *was* more intense from the Ecstasy. And because of the Molly, she stayed horny after she climaxed. The orgasm didn't do anything to sate her desires.

Naeem came (he *nutted*) and ejaculated his black seed into her unprotected pussy like he always did. So far, things were going like all their "*dates.*"

But then, things went ape-shit crazy. And Naeem planned it all. He set up my wife.

Colby arrived at Naeem's house.

"Fuck da bitch, 88," Naeem said to his friend as he pulled out of Kristin's pussy.

"What? What?" Kristin said. Her pretty head was foggy from the Molly and vodka, so she didn't understand what was happening.

Colby sat on the edge of the bed and looked at my almost naked wife. He fondled her big, still perky breasts and caressed her stockinged legs, saying, "God Mrs. Smith, you are so sexy."

Kristin's eyes seemed to focus. It was like she was seeing the star football player for the first time. "What? Colby? What?" she said, still confused.

"It's okay, Mrs. Smith," Colby said as he undressed and got on top of my wife.

"I've wanted to do this for a long time," Colby said as he got between her legs and penetrated her pussy – *bareback* – with his cock.

"Fuck Naeem!" Colby gasped as he pushed his cock into my wife. "She's fucking loose!"

"Yo shoulda fucked da slut at whitey's party," Naeem said with a grin, talking about my son's graduation party. "Da bitch a lot tighter then. I stretched her old bitch cunt. She still fit me good." With a laugh he added, "And yo got a tiny cock anyway 88."

"Fuck you Naeem!" Colby snarled at his friend. But it was true. 88's cock wasn't much bigger than mine.

"It's okay, Mrs. Smith. You still feel good. And you've got a smoking hot body," Colby said as he moved his cock in and out of my wife. He lowered his head and kissed her – and Kristin kissed him back – as he fucked and finally came. He ejaculated his black seed into her, just like Naeem.

Then more black boys arrived. Five or six. They were our son Luke's classmates in high school. They all knew my wife and considered her the sexiest MILF mom of everyone in school. They had lusted Kristin for years, and now they were getting their chance with her.

All the black boys took turns with Kristin. They all fucked her bareback. They all ejaculated their black seed into her.

"I breeding yo, slut," Naeem told Kristin as each of his black brothers pumped their sperm into her. "Yo gonna get fat with nigger baby."

And then things got even worse. It got horrible.

It was late at night, and Naeem and Colby were alone with Kristin. All the other black boys were gone, satiated and happy at having had a go – or two gos for some – with my beautiful wife's sexy body. Some of them took her sexy mouth too.

Kristin was passed out from too much vodka, too much Molly, and too much fucking. She was sleeping in Naeem's bed.

Someone arrived. He was an older, black man, and tattoos covered his body. He was carrying a bag, like a doctor's bag.

"This is her?" the man said, looking down at my sleeping wife.

"Dat da white slut," Naeem confirmed.

The man ran his hand over Kristin's sleeping face. Then he ran his hands over her body. "Pretty face. Nice body," the man said.

"Yo," Naeem said impatiently. "Gonna do this, or what?"

The man looked at Naeem and nodded. "I'm gonna do this, bro. I'm just checking out my canvas." Then the man looked at Kristin's wedding and engagement rings on her left hand. "She's married, huh? To a white man? Her husband's not gonna like this."

"Don't fuckin' care," Naeem said derisively. "Dis cunt is mine. So brand her like we talked."

The older man nodded and opened his bag. He laid out his tools. Needles. Bottles of black ink.

This man was a tattoo artist.

"It's going here, right?" the man said, running a thumb just above Kristin's silky-smooth lily-white skin above her clit. My wife had been completely hairless down there for years, regularly getting waxed.

"Yo right bro," Naeem said, agreeing.

Colby frowned and shook his head. He had known Mrs. Smith for years. He was friends with Luke. Been at their house for dinner lots of times. He said, "I don't know, man. She's passed out. Should we really do this to her? What will Mr. Smith think when he sees it?"

The tattoo artist looked at Colby. "Black is superior to white, my man. You think her husband doesn't know she's fucking Naeem here, and his big cock? He knows. White boys are like that. They're all cuckolds, wanting to see their sweet white wives with black men."

The tattoo artist ran his hand over Kristin's sexy, flat belly. "She's not pregnant, yet?" he asked Naeem.

Naeem shrugged. "Da bitch got nutted with lotsa black seed tonight," he said. "Probably is now."

"You see?" the tattoo artist said to Colby. "Naeem here is a true brother. He doesn't care who breeds this white woman, as long as it's a black brother."

The tattoo artist ran his fingers through Kristin's lush, natural dark blonde hair. He said wishfully, "I *will* miss blonde hair, though, once it's eradicated. Blonde, white girls are hot to fuck." With a grin, he picked up Kristin's left hand with the rings, and added, "Especially blonde girls married to white cuckold husbands." The artist and Naeem laughed. Even Colby grinned. He still liked Luke, but he would never respect Mr. Smith again.

The tattoo artist knew it was only a matter of time before their race's dominate black genes eradicated blonde hair and blue eyes. Eventually, all skin would be different flavors of chocolate. The white race would be no more. And getting there would be fun, with black brothers like Naeem and Colby corrupting young white coeds and stealing white wives from their little dicked white boyfriends and husbands.

Then the tattoo artist when to work. It took some time because he wanted to make it perfect.

When he was done, there was a one-inch high, jet black, Queen of Spades tattoo just above Kristin's clit. Her lily white, smooth, completely unblemished white skin was no more. Now this sexy white MILF was forever branded, marked as black owned.

After he was done, he asked Naeem, "You want me to ink her breasts? Like *Naeem's Property*? Or *Slut for Black Cock*?"

"I don't know," Colby said with a frown. Enough was enough.

Naeem grinned at the idea but shook his head. "Yo right 88. And I like da bitch's tits," he said. "Later maybe, okay bro?"

The tattoo artist shrugged. He knew eventually this MILF's sexy body would be covered with tats. Her white husband won't like it, but he'll probably be history by then. Once white girls like this sexy cougar went black, they never went back.

"Fuck da bitch now, yo," Naeem told the tattoo artist. *Quid pro quo.* He inked her, now he got to fuck her.

The older black man shook his head. "I'll fuck her when her belly's big with a black baby," he said. With a grin, he added, "There's nothing better than fucking a pretty, married white woman in front of her cuckold white husband. Assuming he's still around."

All three black brothers laughed.

————⬤————

KRISTIN WAS BARELY awake when she staggered into her house. She had woken up in Naeem's bed, with her fat, ugly black lover sleeping next to her. She was alarmed and scared waking in the crumbling shack. And she was supposed to be home hours ago. She knew David would be furious. She managed to dress in the dark and hail a taxi. The Molly was still in her system and she didn't trust herself to drive home.

David was awake and worried sick. When Kristin staggered into the house, barely able to stay on her feet, he knew she was drunk. And high – did she take drugs with Naeem?

He carried Kristin to bed. She was only half conscious.

His wife smelled like sex. Lingering in her hair was that distinctive odor of black men. And she reeked of sperm.

David's cock was rock hard. With Kristin barely awake, he pushed up her dress and rammed his cock into her pussy. He wanted to reclaim his wife. He was so frenzied with lust, he didn't see the QoS tattoo above her clit.

Kristin finally woke in the early afternoon. Her head was still foggy from the Molly, and she was hung over from the vodka. She felt dirty from all the sex last night – she didn't remember much, but she knew she'd been fucked by multiple young black men, including Colby. Kristin had never been gangbanged before, and she didn't feel good about it. At the same time, the experience had been amazing! She had cum so many times! So many big black cocks inside her! In her pussy! In her mouth! It had been amazing!

Kristin was still processing what had happened, trying to remember, when she took off her clothes and looked at herself in the mirror. Then she screamed and started to cry. She tried to wash off the QoS tattoo but it wouldn't come off. It was real! It was permanent! Kristin fell to the tile floor in the showered and sobbed uncontrollably.

David was in the family room when he heard his wife scream. He bolted up the stairs to see what was wrong.

⎯⎯⎯⎯⎯●⎯⎯⎯⎯⎯

ONE YEAR LATER

⎯⎯⎯⎯⎯●⎯⎯⎯⎯⎯

I WANTED TO MAKE MY marriage work. Even though she had a QoS tattoo above her clit.

I searched the internet for ways to remove a tattoo. It couldn't be completely removed. There would be a scar there, the remnants of the tat. But Kristin could grow back her pubic hair, a trimmed bush, the way it had been when we first met.

Then we found out she was pregnant. I didn't kid myself; I knew the baby wasn't mine, either Naeem or one of the other black boys had impregnated her. But we could always abort the child. Or give the child up for adoption. Or tell our friends and family we had adopted a black baby.

So, we had options. This could work.

I wanted to stay married to Kristin. I loved her, and despite everything, she was still so beautiful and hot.

But then Kristin told me she was leaving me to be with Naeem. She wasn't sure if she loved the 18-year-old, fat ugly black boy, but this was something she wanted to explore.

My wife of 20 years wanted to explore being *black owned*.

I was devastated. And destroyed. How could she do this to me?

I hired the most cutthroat attorney I could find! I wanted to punish Kristin! I didn't want her to have any of *my* money! I didn't want Naeem to have any of *my* money! *MY MONEY*!!!!

But that's not how divorce works. Kristin got half of everything. *HALF!*

And, I had to pay alimony for 10 years (half the time we were married). Suddenly, Kristin and Naeem – *that fucking nigger!* – were in better financial shape than me. And yes, now I was regularly using the N word.

Kristin went back to work. She was a nurse. With her nurse income, and the alimony I was paying, and half of our wealth, she and Naeem were doing better than me! I was barely able to live! I ended up buying a small RV to live in!

———◉———

TWO YEARS LATER

———◉———

I WAS AT A STARBUCKS when I saw Kristin get in line to order coffee. She still looked good. Really good.

Her face was as beautiful as ever. She had gained a little weight in the hips. Probably from the babies (I heard she got pregnant again after giving birth to the first black baby). But she still looked really good. She was still a sexy MILF.

Kristin saw me. She sat down with her coffee to talk. To catch up.

Our conversation was awkward at first. But I stopped hating her a while ago. And I no longer used the N word. That just wasn't me. And life was short. And she still was the mother of our two children.

"Are you still with Naeem?" I asked.

"Sort of," Kristin said with an embarrassed laugh. "It's more like I'm with a few men now."

"All black?"

Kristin nodded, still looking embarrassed.

"Men? Or boys?" I asked.

Kristin shrugged. "Naeem is 21 now. The others are too. So, I think of them as men."

I looked down at my coffee. My ex was having constant sex with a group of well-hung, black boys (I still thought they were *boys* at 21-years-old – after all, Kristin was 45 now, twice as old as them!).

I barely had a sex life. Sometimes I hooked up with a woman on Tinder, but none were nearly as pretty or sexy as Kristin.

I compared every girl to Kristin. Not one got close to her beauty, or sexiness. I never found any of those meaningless hookups satisfying.

As I was getting ready to leave, Kristin hesitantly asked me, "Have you explored ... you know ... your fantasies?"

I frowned at her. "What do you mean?" I asked, not understanding.

"I mean, David ...," Kristin began. "I think the experience with Naeem taught us both something. For me, my black fantasies from growing up were too strong to resist."

"What did I learn?" I asked, still not understanding.

Kristin looked at me like the answer was obvious. She said, "You're a voyeur. You like watching your wife – your girlfriend – with other men."

I stared at Kristin, dumbstruck. Was she right? I had never connected the dots, but what she said sort of made sense. Was that why my sexual experiences since we broke up were so unsatisfying? Were they too plain vanilla for me?

Kristin reached over the table and took my hand. "I miss you David," she said. She looked sad. "I think about you sometimes. A lot actually."

I was quiet, processing this information. She thought about me?

After a few moments, Kristin asked, "Are you with anyone? Do you have a girlfriend?"

"No," I said honestly. I saw no reason to lie to her.

Kristin smiled looking pleased, and asked, "Do you remember Colby?"

I nodded. Of course I remembered Colby.

"I never knew Naeem back when Luke was growing up," Kristin said. "But Colby was at our house all the time. You know. Hanging out with Luke."

I nodded. I knew this of course. Our son Luke had been good friends with Colby growing up.

Kristin smiled. It was both an embarrassed and wicked smile. She said, "It's kind of sexy – naughty – having sex with Colby. Since I practically helped raise him."

Suddenly my throat was dry. And I was hard in my pants.

"You still have sex with Colby?" I asked, my voice a husky whisper. "Naeem lets you?"

"Naeem doesn't control me. I do whatever I want. We don't live together, you know. In case you're wondering, I don't support him. If you think he gets the money from the divorce, or the alimony, he doesn't. I'm my own girl. I just fuck him sometimes."

I was silent for a moment, processing this information.

"Whenever Colby's home," Kristin said, answering my question. "Yeah, I fuck him. Last night in fact."

A moan escaped my lips. I tried to stop it but couldn't. Kristin heard it and her smile grew bigger.

"We could go to your place," Kristin said. "I could tell you all about it."

"We'd just talk?" I asked.

Kristin smiled again. "Naeem made me get another tat for him," she said. "I'll show it to you." She looked around the crowded Starbucks, and said, "We'll need to be somewhere private for me to show you."

⸺●⸺

SO, THAT'S THE END of my story. I lost my wife to an ugly, fat black kid. But now we're occasional lovers. And occasional friends.

Kristin told me she intentionally gained weight in her hips and ass, because black men think bubble butts are sexy. Her body is amazing!

And her pussy – yes, it's looser now after fucking well hung blacks like Naeem and his friends for years now – but it still feels good to be inside her. And I can still get her off. After all, my cock is about the same size as Colby's, and she gets off with him.

And where is Kristin's second tat that Naeem made her get? And what is it?

Well, that's another story.

MILF SPIES ON NAKED HIGH SCHOOL BOYS

Amy's son Tommy was upset about something. It was really affecting him. Her 18-year-old son had always been a happy boy, but now he seemed depressed. And it was affecting his grades. He had never been an A student, but the last couple of weeks his test grades had dipped into the Cs. He even got a D. When she asked what was wrong, Tommy wouldn't tell her. In fact, he got angry whenever he tried to talk about it.

Then Tommy announced he quit the varsity swimming team. She was shocked. Her son loved swimming. And he even had a chance at a college scholarship for swimming. Amy was very worried about her son.

And Amy was bothered that her husband, Fred, seemed uninterested in their son's plight. But then, Fred had never been a good father, or a good husband. After being married for almost 20 years, the only time he paid attention to her was when he wanted sex. Which was still often, a few times a week.

Fred had always had a high sex drive, but he used to be loving and caring, to both her and their son. Now though, he seemed more interested in ESPN RedZone and his fantasy football teams. And beer. Fred loved exotic IPAs and their drink refrigerator in the basement (her husband's man cave) was full of them.

After being worried sick for weeks, the 40-year-old mother contacted Tommy's high school counselor to try to figure out why Tommy was so upset. His name was Ernie Moore.

The counselor wouldn't talk about Tommy's situation over the phone, "Mrs. Small, this is something we should discuss in person.

Are you available tomorrow afternoon?" Amy immediately agreed. She would move mountains to help her son, so changing her schedule around was nothing to her.

When Amy arrived at the school, Mr. Moore met her at the main school lobby before escorting her to his office. "Wow. She's gorgeous," he thought as Amy introduced herself. She had the bluest blue eyes he had ever seen. She wore little make up – she never did – but the slight coating of lipstick made her pouty lips look soft and moist. She had her blonde hair in a pony tail, and the hairstyle gave her a sweet, innocent look.

The white school counselor purposed trailed behind Amy as they walked to his office. He wanted to look at Amy's figure as they walked. Amy was dressed in office clothes – she had come from work. Mr. Moore liked what he saw. She had a nice ass and long, smooth legs. True, her hips were thicker than the enticing young high school girls at the school, but that was to be expected. Amy was 40-years-old after all, and she had given birth to her son Tommy.

From behind, Mr. Moore could see the outline of Amy's bra strap beneath her white blouse. He saw a panty line in her skirt. Mr. Moore liked seeing a girl's bra strap, but he didn't like seeing a panty line. Clearly Mrs. Small was conservative and didn't wear thongs the way the high school girls did.

Once in his office, Mr. Moore closed the door and ushered Amy into the chair in front of his desk. He took a moment to look at the wife and mother before talking. He saw she had big breasts. He, like most men, liked big breasted women. He wondered if her bra was lacy. Probably not, given the conversative panties she appeared to be wearing under her skirt.

Finally, Mr. Moore took his eyes off Amy's chest and looked into her face. He frowned and said, "Mrs. Small, this is a delicate matter. You see, there have been some pictures that have created a stir here at school.

I can assure you the staff is taking the situation very seriously and when we catch the perpetrator, we will take immediate and serious action."

"Pictures?" Amy was unsure what the counselor was getting at. "What pictures? Can I see them?"

"I'm not sure that would be appropriate," Mr. Moore said with a frown.

Amy felt ready to burst. "If this involves Tommy, then I have a right as his mother to see the pictures!" she demanded.

Mr. Moore's frown deepened but inside he was grinning. He *wanted* to show the pictures to this sexy MILF! He was just enjoying dicking with her!

"Of course, of course," Mr. Moore said, still wearing that fake frown. He pushed some buttons on his keyboard. Then he turned the computer screen, so it was facing Amy. Mr. Moore stood and moved around his desk until he was behind Amy. He did this to ostensibly explain the pictures to Amy. But in fact, he really was hoping to look down the sexy MILF's blouse and see some breast meat, and find out the kind of bra she was wearing.

Amy looked at the picture on the computer screen. She was confused. The picture showed the boys from the varsity swimming team. She recognized them all, since obviously she had gone to all of Tommy's swim meets. In fact, Tommy was in the picture.

Amy more than recognized the boys in the picture. She *knew* these boys well, she'd watched them grow up, because over the years she had chatted with them at swim meets, and they were often at her house hanging out with Tommy.

Amy shook her head and looked confused. "I don't understand," she said. "This is just a picture of the varsity swimming team."

"But you see they're in the locker room," Mr. Moore pointed out.

Amy shrugged. So what? It was not like they were partying with girls. It looked to her this was a picture after practice.

"This isn't the only picture, Mrs. Small," Mr. Moore said. He handed the MILF his wireless keyboard. "You can use the arrow keys to scroll."

The counselor let Mrs. Small be the driver through the pictures on purpose, because he hoped to look down her blouse as she did. And success! The pictures were so shocking, Amy leaned forward to see better, and that caused her blouse to gap. The seedy counselor had a clear view down her blouse!

And Mr. Moore liked what he saw! Amy's breasts were in a bra of course, but he could tell they were big and firm. He was disappointed her bra was plain without any lace or embroidery. But clearly her body was magnificent! Her husband – Mr. Small – was so lucky! He had *this* sexy woman in his bed every night to play with! To fuck!

Amy was shocked as she scrolled through the pictures. They were indeed taken after swim practice. And they showed the boys undressed and showering! The boys of the varsity swim team were naked in some of the pictures!

"These pictures were posted on the internet," Mr. Moore said.

"Oh my god!" Amy gasped. "Now I understand why Tommy's so upset! All the boys must be so upset!"

Mr. Moore shrugged. He said, "Actually, Tommy is the only boy who seems to have a problem with it. The other boys are okay with the pictures on the internet."

Amy stared at the counselor, not understanding. Then she looked back at the pictures, this time studying them more closely.

The swim team boys were obviously unaware that they were being photographed as they casually took off their wet bathing suits, and moved from the showers to their lockers. Amy had seen pornography before – she didn't live under a rock after all. But she had never seen anything so real. Because it *was* real!

And the swim team boys – *oh my!* Their athletic physiques were so muscular and firm. She had seen them in their Speedo swimsuit trunks many times, of course, but seeing them completely naked was an eye opener. *Wow*. All the 18-year-old boys had muscular, well-defined chests, six-pack abs, powerful arms and legs, and tight, muscular butts.

Amy couldn't help comparing the boys' bodies to her husband's. Fred wasn't fat, but his 45-year-old body was flabby and weak by comparison.

Even more than the boys' trim athletic bodies, though, Amy's eyes were drawn to the young men's flaccid penises. She found herself short of breath as she looked at them. They were *so big* compared to her husband's. She never thought her husband's penis was small, but now she saw that it was, at last compared to these boys.

The penises of these young men hung majestically between their muscular legs. She was mesmerized looking at the incredible bodies of these young Adonis's, especially their big cocks. She wondered how big they got when they were aroused. These thoughts made Amy's face heated, and she felt tingling between her legs.

Amy inwardly chastised herself. While it wasn't illegal to look at these naked boys – they were all 18 and some of them were 19, so they were all of legal age – it was certainly inappropriate. Especially since she had watched most of these boys grow up!

But Amy couldn't take her eyes off the pictures. There were only 5, and she found herself scrolling through the 5, and then back again, and back again.

Amy lingered on the 3 pictures that showed the boys' penises. She was shocked the boys were all shaven clean! Amy knew swimmers shaved off their body hair to go faster in the water, but she never imagined they shaved their pubic hair.

That made her wonder – did her son Tommy also shave off his pubic hair? Amy had peripherally seen Tommy in some of the pictures, but had purposely avoided focusing on him, not wanting to look at her naked son.

Amy scrolled back to the 3 pictures that showed the boys' penises. She saw Tommy *was* in the picture.

Amy looked at her naked son. She was proud to see he had the same firm, muscular physique of all the other boys on the varsity swim team.

But when Amy lowered her eyes – she had to force herself - she saw that Tommy's penis was small, especially compared to the other boys. And she recognized his size. Tommy's soft penis was almost the same size as her husband Fred's penis when he was soft.

"Poor Tommy," Amy thought as she looked at her naked son. "You inherited your father's penis size."

And then Amy understood why her Tommy was so upset. The entire school – all the girls! – now knew Tommy had a small penis. And she understood why he quit the swim team. Tommy was a fast swimmer, he had some of the best times in their district, but he couldn't compete with the other boys on the swim team in the one area that meant most to boys – the size of their cocks!

Amy felt sadness for her son, but she still couldn't take her eyes off the pictures. She suddenly had the naughty desire to put faces to cocks. She was intensely curious to see the penises of the boys on the team she knew best!

Amy carefully studied the 3 photos that shown the fronts of the boys. That showed their faces *and* their cocks.

She noticed Billy, who vacationed with her family two summers ago. His body was muscular and smooth, like a movie star. Amy knew Billy was 19-years-old, and that made her feel a little less guilty about looking at him. Her eyes focused on Billy's penis. It was soft, of course, but noticeably bigger than Tommy's (and her husband's).

Then Amy looked at Jeffrey, another 19-year-old. *Oh my!* His cock was even larger than Billy's, and uncircumcised! Amy had butterflies. She had never seen an uncircumcised penis in real life.

All the boys looked so powerful and masculine with their tight, muscular bodies and their big cocks. All except for her poor Tommy.

And her husband Fred – he didn't even have their son's muscular body. Her husband had never been an athlete, but the last few years he had let himself go with too much beer and fantasy football. Now her husband's body was soft and pudgy, and on top of that, now Amy knew he had a small penis.

For long moments, Amy's attention was drawn to Bobby, one of the 18-year-old boys on the team. Bobby was the best swimmer on the team – and the district – and probably it was because of his tall frame (he was well over 6 feet), broad shoulders, powerful arms and legs, and washboard abs. Bobby was not in the 3 pictures showing the boys' fronts, and she was disappointed. Amy would have liked to see his front – to see his penis.

Mr. Moore, the counselor, watched Amy as she looked through the pictures. Her face was flushed and her breathing shallow. The beautiful MILF's nipples were hard and denting her bra and blouse. Sexual tension was in the air, and the counselor's cock got hard in his pants.

Amy finally tore her eyes from the pictures. She forced herself back into mom mode.

"How were these pictures taken?" she demanded.

"There's a storeroom next to the boy's locker room," Mr. Moore said. "Someone made a pin-hole and used it to take pictures of the boys. As we said, we will find out who that was, and punishment will be severe."

Amy nodded. Her face still felt hot, and that special place between her legs throbbed. She abruptly stood and hurried away from Mr. Moore's office.

Later that night, Fred wanted sex as he often did. This time Amy welcomed his advances. She was so horny!

But she didn't orgasm from sex with her husband. She rarely did. And now she knew why. Fred's body was not at all sexy. And his cock was small.

God, how ironic! Her husband's last name – and now her last name – was *Small*! But Amy knew the joke was on her, as all she had in her bed was a husband with a little dick.

The next day, Amy took the day off from work. Once she was alone in the house – after Fred went to work and Tommy to school – Amy got into bed with her computer.

The pictures of the swim team boys were at a private website. Amy had memorized the URL and password that were scrawled on a sticky note on the counselor's computer screen.

Amy got undressed, then she navigated to that website. She played with herself as she looked at the naked boys. With one hand she fondled one of her big tits. With the other she played with her pussy and clit. It felt so good touching herself while looking at the muscular, manly naked bodies of these young men!

Then Amy focused on the picture of Bobby and his tall, muscular body. Unfortunately, he was only in two of the five pictures, and none showed his front. Still, seeing the back of his powerful body, especially his firm muscular behind, and his handsome face turned Amy on more than any of the other boys. Her eyes moving from Bobby's face, down his muscular back, and then his beautiful ass, Amy had an enormous orgasm.

Over the next month, Amy became obsessed with the pictures of the young, naked 18-and 19-year-old boys. She masturbated to the pictures every day, sometimes at work in the bathroom. She became especially obsessed with Bobby, always cumming when she looked at the pictures of him.

God! Amy so wished there were pictures of Bobby's front! She desperately wished she could see his naked cock!

Amy became so obsessed with the idea of seeing more of Bobby, that she found herself in the counselor's office again. She had noticed the counselor leering at her when she was here before, and had dressed a bit sexy, hoping her female charms might entice the counselor to agree to her request.

Amy wasn't physically attracted to this counselor. Mr. Moore was balding and fat. He made her husband look like a movie star by comparison!

But, if wearing a tighter blouse, a shorter skirt, sexy bra and panties, stockings and heels would help her get what she wanted, then it would be worth it. He could look all he wanted as long as she got what she was here for.

"How can I help you, Mrs. Small?" the counselor asked as he openly stared at the MILF's chest.

Amy arched her back, inviting the creepy counselor to leer at her. "I heard you caught the person," the wife and mother said.

"Yes, Mrs. Small," the counselor said. "A freshman. A very bad girl, especially given her young age. Of course, she has been expelled."

"Did she have any more pictures?" Amy asked, trying to keep her excitement out of her voice. If there were more pictures, then she might see Bobby in all his glory!

"No," Mr. Moore said. "Fortunately, there were no more pictures."

"Yes. That's good," Amy said, looking defeated. She couldn't keep the disappointment out of her voice. No more pictures. No more pictures of naked Bobby. She would never see his cock. Amy felt like crying. She had so pinned her hopes on there being more pictures.

Mr. Moore heard the disappointment in Amy voice, and in her face. He read her like a book. After all, he *was* a school counselor. He did have *some* skill at his job, and often it was important to discern the truth in what students said, which were often lies.

"This unfortunate incident is not quite over," Mr. Moore said. "We haven't closed the pinhole in that closet. That will happen tomorrow. The door has been locked, though, so no one has had access to that pinhole into the boy's locker room."

"Oh," Amy said, suddenly interested in what this fat, ugly man was saying.

"I have the only key," Mr. Moore said. "Would you like to see the closet, the pinhole? It's the scene of the crime. For closure for you and your son Tommy?"

Then the fat counselor looked at his watch. "Maybe this isn't a good time. Swim practice is just ending. The boys will be undressing, and showering."

Amy saw her chance! Her only chance to see all of Bobby's naked body! To see his cock!

"Actually Mr. Moore, I think this is the perfect time," she hurriedly said.

"Of course," Mr. Moore said with a big eager grin. "And please Mrs. Small. Call me Ernie. Can I call you Amy?"

⸻●⸻

ERNIE AND AMY QUICKLY walked to the closet. Luckily, school was over, so they didn't see anyone in the hallways.

Ernie unlocked the door, and they quickly went inside. The counselor locked the door from the inside. Since he had the only key, no one could disturb them.

"Over there," Ernie whispered, motioning to the wall at the end of the storeroom. Amy hurriedly walked over, her high heels click-clacking on the cheap tile floor. She found the pinhole. Holding her breath, she looked through the hole.

Oh my.

OH MY GOD!

The 18- and 19-year-old boys on the varsity swim team were naked! Their bodies were amazing! Their youthful, handsome faces were gorgeous!

It was amazing seeing them in person! It was like watching a movie! No, better than a movie! This was real!

Amy searched for Bobby! He was the only one she cared about! She wanted to see Bobby's naked body!

She saw him! But his back was to her!

"Turn around!" Amy silently begged. *"Bobby, please turn around! Please!"*

And then he did. Bobby turned around.

Amy saw his front. His naked front.

She saw his penis.

"OH – MY – GOD!" she whispered. It was *SO* big!

Bobby's penis was the biggest of all the boys! Even soft, his cock was the longest, and it was so thick! How could he possibly stuff that monster into his Speedos?!

Amy knew that the creepy counselor was in the storeroom with her. But she began touching herself as she looked at Bobby. At his handsome face. At his powerful body. At his magnificent manhood.

She knew that Mr. Moore was watching her, but she didn't care! This was her *only* chance to masturbate looking at Bobby! If creepy Ernie jerked off looking at her, then she didn't care!

Then Amy felt Ernie behind her. He pressed his fat stomach against her back. His hand was suddenly touching her breast. His other hand was under her skirt.

"Keep watching Amy," Ernie hissed into her ear. "You get what you want. And I get what I want."

Then Ernie was opening her blouse and unsnapping her bra. And he was pulling up her skirt and pulling down her pantyhose and thong panties.

Amy heard the distinct sound of a zipper opening. And then she felt Ernie's hard cock pressing against her womanhood.

"Keep watching those naked boys, Amy," Ernie hissed into her ear. He pushed away her hand that had been frigging her clit through her pantyhose and thong.

"I'll do this for you," Ernie said as he pushed his cock into Amy's married pussy.

Amy was a faithful wife. She had never cheated before. But now another man's cock was inside her.

The cock of a fat, ugly, creepy man.

But it felt good! Ernie's cock was big! Much longer and thicker than her husband's!

Amy let Ernie fucked her as she watched through the pinhole. As she focused on Bobby and his naked body. On the 18-year-old's big cock.

Amy wished it was Bobby fucking her, instead of Ernie. But she had to admit, the fat, ugly man knew how to fuck. Soon Amy was cumming. Ernie had to cover her mouth with his pudgy fingers to stop her from screaming.

Amy couldn't remember the last time her husband Fred had made her cum from intercourse! And this had been an amazing orgasm! Maybe the best orgasm of her life!

Ernie wasn't going to last much longer. This was the fuck of his life! Amy's body was so firm for a woman her age, and her breasts heavy and shapely. And her pussy exquisite! So tight! Her husband must have a tiny pencil dick for her pussy to be so tight after being married as long.

Moments later, Amy head Ernie growl and lurch. She knew he was about to orgasm. She didn't want him to cum inside her, but she couldn't fight as the boys would hear.

Amy felt Ernie cum! She felt him ejaculate inside her! He came so much and so forcefully, she felt his sperm hit her walls!

After they were done, Amy hoped the creepy, fat counselor had not just gotten her pregnant. She wasn't on any birth control. Her husband Fred always used condoms.

———⊸●⊷———

A COUPLE WEEKS LATER, Mr. Moore called Bobby into his office.

"Am I in trouble?" Bobby asked warily. "If something gets on my record, it could screw up my scholarship." The star swimmer had scholarship offers from a lot of schools, but he was focused on the University of Miami because of South Beach. And the blonde, bikini-clad girls.

"No, no," Mr. Moore said amicably. "You're not in any trouble Bobby. I just have a proposition for you."

"A proposition, huh?" Bobby said guardedly. As a swimmer with a handsome face and stud body, he got hit on by fags a lot. He wasn't interested at all, as Bobby was all man.

Bobby didn't want to be hit on by Mr. Moore. But guidance counselor could easily put something fake into his record. That would fuck up his college dreams.

Bobby asked himself, *"Would I suck this man's dick or let him fuck me in the ass to get into the college I want?"*

But Mr. Moore didn't seem like a fag. Bobby saw the fat, balding guidance counselor leering at the cheerleaders in their tiny skirts as much as him.

"So, Bobby, have you done well with the girls, since the pictures got out?" Mr. Moore asked with a friendly smile. "That is, after all the girls saw how big your dick is?"

Bobby frowned at the counselor. Where was he going with this?

Bobby shrugged and said, "I've done okay."

Mr. Moore continued to smile. "You're being modest. From what I hear, you're very popular with the girls. Especially after the pictures got posted."

"From what you hear?" Bobby said with a distasteful look. This guidance counselor was a serious pervert. Bobby did not like this fat, balding man.

"And not just with students," Mr. Moore said. "With some of the moms, too."

"What do you mean?" Bobby said, suddenly interested. "What moms?"

"One in particular," Mr. Moore said. His grin was even bigger now. He knew he had this kid hooked. "You know Tommy's mother?"

"Mrs. Small?" Bobby said, looking shocked and incredulous. Mrs. Small was the prettiest and sexiest of all the moms! The hottest MILF in the state!

Mrs. Small saw the pictures? *She* was interested in him?

"How would you like to have sex with Mrs. Small?" the counselor asked. "I'll set it up."

"You'll set it up?" Bobby asked guardedly. "And what do *you* get?"

"Nothing from you, my boy, nothing from you," Mr. Moore assured the handsome swimmer. "Just don't say anything after."

Bobby shrugged. Of course, he wouldn't say anything. Mrs. Small was married. He liked her. He wanted to fuck her, yes, but he didn't want to screw up her marriage. And anyway, her son Tommy was his friend. They had been friends since grade school. He had known Mrs. Small since grade school. He had jerked off many times fantasizing about Tommy's mother. And now he was going to get to fuck her? Really?

"Just do as I say," Mr. Moore told the 18-year-old swimmer. "And you'll have your fun with Mrs. Small."

⸺●⸺

AMY WAS SCARED WHEN she knocked on Mr. Moore's door at school. He called her yesterday and asked her to stop by. They hadn't spoken since what happened in the storeroom.

"Come in, come in," Mr. Moore said happily. He ushered her to the chair in front of his desk. Then he sat in the chair behind his desk.

"Mr. Moore, what do you want?" Amy asked looking scared. She knew this vile man had power over her. She had given into her lusts and looked at the naked boys of the varsity swim team. And he had fucked her. Was he going to blackmail her for money? Or even worse, for more sex? Had there been a secret camera in the storeroom? Amy knew if he had video, the counselor could ruin her life. She might even go to jail.

"Amy, you look scared," the counselor said with a friendly smile. "I'm not going to hurt you, or threaten you. And it's Ernie, remember?"

"Then what do you want?" Amy said, still looking guarded. Knowing it would be good to appease the fat, balding man, she added, "Ernie."

The counselor looked happy the sexy MILF called him by his first name. "Amy, I think we can work something out. A win-win."

"What do you mean?"

"I think I know the boy you're interested in," Ernie said. "Bobby, right? It's a guess, but a good guess I think. All the schoolgirls want Bobby. And I see mothers at swim meets checking out his body. So, it's Bobby, right? You fantasize about him, right? I bet you were looking at him when you orgasmed in the storeroom. On my cock, by the way, so I do take some of the credit for that."

Amy's cheeks flushed red with embarrassment, and humiliation. Where was he going with this? Anyways, there was no way she was going to admit anything! He might be recording this conversation!

"I don't know what you're talking about," Amy said. Ernie smiled. He knew she was lying.

"How would you like that young man to fuck you?" Ernie asked. "To feel his young hard body on top of you? To feel his big, youthful cock inside you? Would you want that, Amy?"

Amy's cheeks got even redder, but now it was arousal. She had fantasized many times about Bobby while masturbating, both before and after what happened in the storage closet. But again, she wasn't stupid enough to admit anything.

"I don't know what you're talking about," she said again.

"It would be completely safe for you," Ernie assured her. "Bobby won't know it's you. He won't be able to see your face. The room will be completely dark. All he'll know is he's with a sexy mom of one of his friends. You'll be able to have Bobby, experience him, and he'll never know it's you."

Amy stared at Ernie. She was breathing hard, and her heart was pounding. Was it possible? Could she have sex with the boy she lusted after, without any consequences?

But there *would* be consequences. Ernie wouldn't go to the trouble of setting this up without getting something.

"And what do you get?" Amy asked. Although she was pretty sure she already knew.

"I get you," Ernie said simply, a big lecherous grin on his fat face. "After Bobby is done with you, I get my turn. With the lights on, of course. The storeroom fuck was great, but I didn't get to see your body, or touch you properly, or kiss you. I want to see your pretty face Amy, and kiss you, while we fuck. So, what do you say? You get Bobby's body. And I get yours. Do you agree?"

Amy stared at Ernie for a long time. Finally, she nodded her head yes.

⸺●⸺

BOBBY KNOCKED AND THEN walked into Mr. Moore's apartment. "Is she here?" the 18-year-old high school senior asked.

"In my bedroom. She's already naked," the guidance counselor said. "It's dark. You won't be able to see each other. She thinks you don't know who she is. You can talk to her. She knows who *you* are. But don't let on you know who she is."

"I don't get it. I'm not supposed to know who she is?" Bobby asked. He might be a champion swimmer, but he wasn't the brightest kid.

The guidance counselor was used to dealing with dumb jocks like Bobby. He patiently explained, "That's the only way she would do this. If you don't know who she is, you can't tell anyone about fucking her. So, she thinks she's safe. She thinks you know it's one of your friend's moms, not which mom. She thinks this is a taboo fantasy for both of you. She gets to fuck a young, virile high school student. And you get to fuck one of your friend's moms, a MILF.

Bobby slowly nodded as the lightbulb in his head finally came on. "Okay, I get it," he said. "But then why did you tell me it's Mrs. Small?"

Mr. Moore grinned and said, "Because it makes it hotter for you if you *know* it's Mrs. Small, right?"

"Fucking-A," Bobby said in agreement. He grinned at the guidance counselor. He liked this man!

"So, what do you get out of this?" Bobby asked.

"I think you know," Mr. Moore said with a grin at the young man. "Once you're done with Amy, I get my turn with her."

Bobby laughed. He definitely liked this man! His friend Tommy's mom getting fucked twice by men not her husband! This was the hottest moment of his life!

"And maybe some time, you can return the favor," Mr. Moore said. "Those pretty high school cheerleaders you get into your bed. Maybe you can do this set up for me sometimes."

"Okay, yeah, I can do that," Bobby said with another laugh. What did he care if those cheerleaders got banged by this fat old man? It's not like he was gonna marry any of them.

A moment later, Mr. Moore turned off all the lights in his apartment. With the apartment completely dark, Bobby went into the bedroom. Mr. Moore went in too. He wouldn't be able to see anything, but he wanted to listen.

AMY FELT BUTTERFLIES in her stomach as a male body got onto the bed with her.

"Hi Mrs. Somebody," she heard a voice say. She recognized it. It was Bobby! This was really going to happen!

Bobby found Amy's breasts in the darkness and fondled them. "I know you know I'm Bobby. I know you're one of my friends' mom," he said. "I'm gonna really enjoy this. I've got a thing for MILFs. And I can tell you've got a rocking body."

Amy moaned as Bobby fondled her breasts. She was tempted to tell Bobby who she was, so he would know it was *her* – Amy Small—who has that *rocking* body. But good sense prevailed. She couldn't let Bobby know it was Tommy's mom who he was about to fuck.

But she could touch this 18-year-old's body, and that's what she did. As Bobby caressed her, she caressed him. She touched his chiseled chest, his powerful arms, his muscular legs ... she traced his hard, well-defined muscles with her fingertips.

OH MY GOD! Bobby's 18-year-old body was so amazing! His body was incredible!

She imagined what it would be like to have Bobby in her bed every night. His hard body, instead of her husband's soft, flabby body. Feeling Bobby's steel hard pecs, instead of her husband's man boobs.

"Can I ask you something, Mrs. Somebody?" Bobby asked. His hands were roving over her breasts and flat sexy tummy. "I guess we know each other, right? We've talked?"

Bobby moved his hand to Amy's face. He felt her nod her head yes.

"God that's so hot!" Bobby said enthusiastically. "So, do you have a thing for me? Have you masturbated thinking of me?"

Amy hesitated. It was an embarrassing thing to admit to. But he didn't know who she was, which *mom* she was, so she nodded her head yes again.

"Oh fuck! That is so hot! I wish I knew who you were! I *could* say who I *hope* you are, the mom who I jerk off to the most, but I don't want to hurt your feelings if you're not her."

Amy's heart leaped in her chest! Was it possible? Did this hot, gorgeous boy fantasize about *her*?

Bobby was still talking. He asked, "Do moms look at our cocks in the Speedos, at meets?"

Bobby again moved his hand to Amy's face in the darkness. He felt the MILF nod her head yes.

He chuckled. "Do moms volunteer to time, to get a better view of our cocks?" he asked. Volunteer timers at swim meets stood at the pool's edge, right next to the blocks where the swimmers dived in from.

Bobby chuckled when he felt Amy nod her head yes again.

"Is that why you set this up with Mr. Moore? Because you saw my bulge in the Speedos?"

Amy nodded. The size of the bulge in the Speedos wasn't the only reason. Other reasons were his amazing, god-like body, and his very handsome face. Amy admitted to herself that maybe she had a little crush on this young man. Which was crazy and so wrong, since she was literally old enough to be his mother.

Bobby took Amy's hand and moved it to his cock. Like her, he was completely naked.

"Does the reality live up to your fantasies?" Bobby asked as Amy touched his cock for the first time.

Amy moaned. His cock was so big! So long and thick! So hard! So masculine!

Bobby said, "You've got a smoking hot body," as he caressed Amy's tits, her flat belly, her ass, her legs. This was *Mrs. Small!* The hottest mom! The hottest MILF! He had lusted after her for year! He had jerked off to her for years!

Bobby was just as excited to be with Amy, as she was with him!

And after tonight, Mrs. Small would no longer be a fantasy! She would be another notch in his belt!

He grinned. It got him hot thinking about his friend Tommy's mom as his slut! As his cum bucket!

Bobby moved between Amy's open legs in the darkness. "I'm about to fuck you, Mrs. Somebody. Have you ever cheated on your husband before?"

Bobby moved his hand to her face and felt Amy shake her head no. In reality, she *had* cheated on Fred when Ernie took her in the storeroom. But that wasn't really cheated. Amy wasn't attracted at all to the guidance counselor. He had just taken advantage of an opportunity.

"Good," Bobby said. "I like being your first. It's like I'm taking your virginity. Think about it, Mrs. Somebody. An 18-year-old boy taking your faithfulness and making your husband a cuckold."

Amy moaned. The nastiness of Bobby's words were so delicious! How could this teenager be so skilled at pushing her erotic buttons?

"Here we go, Mrs. Somebody," Bobby said. "In a second, you won't be a faithful wife anymore. You'll be a cheating wife."

Amy moaned again, and as she did, Bobby pushed his cock into her married pussy.

"Oh god!" Amy said. She wasn't supposed to say anything as Bobby might recognize her voice, but she couldn't help it. The 18-year-old was so big! So thick! She had never had a cock so big inside her!

"Fuck, Mrs. Somebody, you are seriously tight!" Bobby grunted as he struggled to penetrate the married MILF's pussy with his big cock.

Amy grimaced as Bobby pushed into her, inch by inch. It was painful. But felt so good too!

Then Bobby began fucking Amy. Slowly at first, and then faster and harder. Amy came almost immediately, screaming as her orgasm hit. The pleasure was so intense she saw bright fireworks in the dark room.

Soon after, Bobby was cumming. Usually he was able to last longer, but this MILF's pussy felt so good! So tight! He knew at that moment that Mrs. Small's husband had a tiny dick, just like their son Tommy.

"Fuck!" Bobby screamed as he came and ejaculated into Amy.

Amy felt Bobby's virile sperm splashing against her walls. She still wasn't on birth control. Luckily she hadn't gotten pregnant when the guidance counselor came inside her in the storage room.

She didn't care if Bobby got her pregnant, though. She would be honored to carry the baby of this 18-year-old godlike boy.

After, Bobby pulled out of Amy and quickly left. The deal was, he had a turn with Tommy's mom, and then it was Mr. Moore's turn.

Tommy hoped Mr. Moore would set him up with other MILFs. None of them were nearly as pretty and sexy as Mrs. Small, but still, it would be hot to fuck more of his friends' moms. So he was going to obey Mr. Moore's rules to stay on his good side.

Amy was disappointed when Tommy pulled out and left. It was over too fast. Much too fast.

She realized she didn't kiss Bobby. She had so wanted to kiss the gorgeous 18-year-old. She felt like crying after missing out on her one opportunity to kiss him.

Mr. Moore turned on the lights when the teenager was gone. He looked at Amy.

This was his first time seeing her naked. Her body was magnificent! And her face so pretty, and extra sexy with her hair messed up after the fucking she just got from Bobby.

"Amy, your body is really something," the fat, sleazy guidance counselor said as he leered at her naked MILF body. He wasn't able to wait. He quickly got into bed with Tommy's mother and rammed his cock into her.

Mr. Moore went balls deep into Amy's body easily. Bobby had stretched her out.

Mr. Moore fucked her hard and fast.

Mr. Moore moved to kiss Amy as he fucked her. She turned her head, saying, "Mr. Moore—."

"I *told* you to call me Ernie."

"Ernie," Amy said. "You can fuck me. But no kissing." The last thing the married woman wanted was to kiss this vile, fat man. Especially after missing on her chance to kiss the *Adonis* Bobby.

"That wasn't our deal, Amy," Ernie said as he covered the MILF's lips with his and kissed her. Ernie pushed his tongue down Amy's throat and she practically gagged. His mouth tasted like disgusting cigarettes and left-over meatloaf (which had been his dinner earlier).

Finally, Ernie came, adding his spunk to Bobby's. Amy hadn't cum close to cumming. Ernie didn't compare to Bobby. Not even close. After just being with Bobby, there was no chance she would orgasm with the fat, balding guidance counselor.

Amy quickly dressed and was about to go, when Ernie said, "We can do this again."

"What?"

"I can set you up with other boys," Ernie said. "Just like this."

Amy stared at Ernie. She was tempted. To regularly have sex with fit, teenage boys. It would be so much better than her flabby husband at home, with his little dick.

But Amy shook her head no. It wasn't because of morals. At this point, she didn't care about the sin of having sex with young boys, as long as they were legal. But fucking those boys meant she would also have to let this disgusting man fuck her. And that she would never do. Not again.

"No, Mr. Moore," Amy said with finality.

"Call me Ernie," he said.

Amy shook her head no again. She would never call him Ernie again. If she had her way, she would never speak to him again.

It was lucky Amy told Ernie no. Because he planned for the next teenage boy to be her son, Tommy. With Tommy though, he would not reveal which mom he would get to fuck.

In the darkness, the mother would not find out until after, that her son had fucked her. The idea of this sexy MILF getting fucked by her son she obviously adored turned on the sleazy guidance counselor. And the cherry on the top was, Amy probably wouldn't get an orgasm out of the incest fucking, since Tommy had a little dick.

"Too bad," Ernie said to himself when Amy was gone. But he knew there were other sexy moms out there who were sexually frustrated. Maybe he could corrupt another MILF, just like he had with Amy.

EPILOGUE - ONE YEAR Later

TOMMY WAS WITH HIS high school buddies at his house. Everyone was home for the summer and the friends were hanging together.

Bobby was there, and Amy tried to avoid the young man (now he was 19-years-old). But for a few moments they were alone in the basement as Tommy and his other friends went upstairs for snacks.

Bobby sat next to Amy. He put his hand on her knee and whispered, "I know it was you."

Amy immediately sputtered, "Bobby, what are you talking about?"

"It's okay Mrs. Small," Bobby said reassuringly. "I haven't told anyone. I'll never tell anyone."

Bobby squeezed Amy's knee and said, "I'm home all summer. You want to do it again? This time with the lights on? You are seriously the most beautiful, sexiest girl I've ever been with. And yeah – you're the mom I jerk off to. I've fantasized about you for years."

Amy's head was spinning – exploding! – with what Bobby was saying.

And at that moment, she knew she would get another chance to kiss this youthful, gorgeous, sexy boy. But when?

"When?" Amy whispered.

Bobby grinned. Now he was certain he was getting into Mrs. Small's pants again. This time with the lights on!

"No time like the present," the 19-year-old said.

Amy's heart leaped! He wants me so much, he can't wait! She felt like a teenager again after a boy she liked just gave her a compliment.

But then Amy remembered. "We can't tonight," she whispered, disappointment in her voice. "I'm not on the pill. Unless you have a condom?"

Amy knew she was lucky not to get pregnant after both Mr. Moore and Bobby came inside her. She had to be more careful. She decided at that moment to go back on the pill. But it would take some time before the pill was working and protecting her against pregnancy.

Bobby's eyes opened wide with shock. "Mrs. Small's not on the pill?" he thought to himself. "How could that be?"

But then, Bobby had seen Mr. Small's pudgy body in his bathing suit a few times, and he probably had a little dick just like Tommy. So maybe there was no need for Mrs. Small to be protected because she never fucked her husband. He didn't know Fred always used condoms with his wife. The last thing he wanted was another brat kid, and he liked his wife's body just the way it was, curvy like a woman should be, but also tight and firm.

Bobby had a condom in his wallet, but he wanted to fuck Mrs. Small bareback. "I'll pull out," he promised.

Amy looked down at her feet as she thought about it. She wanted Bobby – now! She didn't want to wait!

She could try one of her husband's condoms, but she knew they were too small for the well-hung teenager. And Bobby had just promised to pull out ....

"How will we do this?" Amy asked Bobby. Even though she was much older, Bobby had way more experience with hooking up with girls.

"I'll tell Tommy I'm going home," Bobby said. "You tell everyone you're going to bed. And then I'll meet you in your bedroom. Mr. Small's not home, right?"

Amy nodded. Her husband Fred was away for the weekend with friends, a boy's vacation.

Amy shivered at Bobby's plan. She was going to let this teenage boy fuck her in her marital bed, with her son Tommy and his friends downstairs. The idea was so naughty, so wicked – *so wrong!* – it made her knees weak and her pussy throb.

"Okay," Amy whispered, and they both smiled conspiratorially at each other.

Of course, Bobby was lying. He had no intention of pulling out. He planned to fuck Mrs. Small and ejaculate his seed into her unprotected pussy as much as possible before she wised up and went on birth control.

Bobby wanted to impregnant Mrs. Small. His greatest fantasy was to breed girls. And the chance to breed Mrs. Small, this sexy MILF, this sexy wife, his friend Tommy's mom ... Bobby was *not* going to let this opportunity slip by.

"I hope she's ovulating," he thought to himself.

"Can I call you Amy?" the teenager asked.

Amy nodded yes. She didn't realize the choices she was making tonight were going to change her life. It would lead to pregnancy. It would lead to divorce. It would lead to scandal. It would ruin her life.

At that moment, though, Amy only cared about feeling Bobby's big cock inside her again.

And having the light on so she could look at his handsome teenager face and wonderful teenager body as he stroked his cock inside her.

And kissing him.

THE GIRL WHO USED TO BABYSIT ME

I was 28-years-old at a Starbucks with my nose in my phone, scrolling through the job listings at Indeed. I'd just gotten laid off and needed a new job ASAP to make rent. I'd been an honor student in high school and college, but my career was not going well. The fucking economy! In the 6 years since graduation, I'd been laid off 4 times!

I noticed a woman in a dark business suit walk into the Starbucks. She got in line to order.

"Wow, nice legs," I thought to myself. Looking at her back, her ass and hips were a little thick, but her legs in the dark nylons and black high heels were amazing.

I was better with the girls than my career. I was good looking and fit, and I had a pretty good package in my pants. Unfortunately, being good in bed wasn't something I could put on my resume.

The woman turned around. She was an older woman. Probably in her 40s. She had an attractive face, although the wrinkles around her eyes and lips showed her age. She looked sad too, which probably didn't help with her wrinkles.

I saw she was petite. In her starched white blouse, she looked to have small breasts. Her stomach noticeably bulged against her blouse and skirt, so I guessed she carried some unwanted weight there. Probably she'd gone through one or two pregnancies and had never been able to get her flat belly back (assuming she ever had one).

The woman looked familiar so I looked at her for long moments. Then I put a name to the face. It was Emma! She used to be my nanny when I was a kid!

That was years ago. More than 20 years. Back then, I'd been a bratty grade schooler and she had just graduated from college.

Emma had been my first childhood crush. Back then, she'd been a bubbly young college grad with a pretty face, slim body, little tits and long, incredible legs. She was doing the nanny thing for a few years while she figured out what she wanted to do in life.

As a kid, I adored Emma! And I lusted after her! She was the first girl – the only girl – I fantasized about when I began masturbating. She left after a few years to chase her dreams, and I eventually forgot about her as I grew up and began having real sex with girls my age. But as I looked at her standing in line, I realized I still had a fondness in my heart for her.

I went up to Emma and told her who I was. She was shocked to see me, but happy too. She looked a lot prettier and youthful when she smiled.

We sat down with our coffees and caught up. My story took only a few minutes to tell. I was 28, I went to good schools and got good grads, but the economy was shitty and I just got laid off – again!

Emma said nice things to me, about how she always thought I was so smart and I'd land on my feet eventually. I felt like she was being honest and not just being nice. I found myself feeling an even more fondness for my old nanny.

Emma's story took longer to tell. After she stopped being my nanny, she started a marketing company and she still worked there, as the CEO. It was doing well, although it was a small company.

She got married to a handsome successful man and had two children. Her life had been perfect, like a Disney movie. But then her husband William cheated on her with a much younger woman. And he cheated again. And again.

When she decided enough was enough and asked for a divorce, William was cruel to her. He told her he cheated because he was no longer attracted to her. He said she wasn't pretty anymore, her tits sagged, she was fat and had a loose pussy. No one would blame him for upgrading to a younger, prettier, tighter girl.

That was 3 years ago, and Emma admitted she had not had sex with anyone since then. Even before the divorce, she knew she was no longer pretty and desirable like she had been when she was younger. Childbirth, raising children, and the stress of running her own company took a tool on a woman's looks and body.

But the terrible, harsh words of her ex-husband when he spoke to her for the last time really destroyed her confidence and self-image. Especially now at 43 years old. She felt her ex-husband had used her all up, and now there wasn't anything left in her for sex, much less romance.

I couldn't believe William! How could any man be such a dick?

As our stories ended, and with our coffee cups empty, Emma looked at me. She said, "You've become a really handsome man, Mikey."

I laughed. "No one's called me Mikey in years. Not even my parents."

"Oh. Sorry," Emma said with an embarrassed grin.

Emma ran her eyes from my face and down my body. In my adult life, I had seen many girls look that way at me. Like I said, I was a handsome, fit man. Girls looked at me like that all the time.

Emma invited me to dinner for Saturday. At her house. She would cook me a home meal, just like when she used to be my nanny.

I almost declined. I knew if I went to her house, she might hit on me. And then things would get really awkward. Because while Emma had been my first crush and stroke fantasy, this wasn't the 21-year-old Emma from so long ago. Back then she had been so pretty and hot, so ripe. But this 43-year-old woman wasn't like that anymore. While I thought her ex-husband's parting words had been cruel, they might be more true than false.

But I couldn't refuse. This woman already had shaky confidence and self-esteem. If I said no, it would be *me* being the cruel dick. And anyway, Emma wasn't going to hit on me. She used to be my nanny after all, she was 15 years older, and she was the prim and proper CEO of her own company.

That Saturday I went to her house. It was a condo actually, in an expensive building in one of the affluent parts of the city. I figured Emma's company must be doing pretty good if she could afford to live in this place.

Emma was dressed casually. Just a t-shirt and shorts, and in bare feet, with her hair in a ponytail. The way she looked kind of reminded me of Emma when she was my 21-year-old nanny.

After dinner, we sat on her sofa as we finished our wine. I saw Emma looking at me, and stealing glances at my chest and my crotch.

Then I noticed dents in Emma's t-shirt. Her nipples were hard and were denting her t-shirt! Had my old nanny gone braless?!

I looked at Emma's face. Her cheeks were flushed. Her eyes heavy lidded.

I'd seen that look many times on chicks. Emma was aroused.

So, I wasn't a kid anymore and Emma wasn't a 21-year-old hottie. I wasn't attracted to her.

But she was my friend. And she was down on her luck love-wise, just like I was down career-wise.

Would it be that bad if I had sex with her? I mean, the idea of fucking my old nanny was sort of exciting in a kinky way. And Emma's legs looked fantastic in those shorts. And I saw her feet were very pretty.

I leaned in and kissed Emma. I fondled her. I undressed her.

I was in control. Even though she was 15 years older, Emma had been too devastated by her ex-husband to be anything but a passive participate.

Once she was naked, Emma stood up like she wanted to run away. She looked scared and shyly covered her breasts with her hands. "I'm sorry Mikey," she said, regret in her voice. "I know you used to have a crush on me. I'm sorry I'm not pretty the way I used to be."

Emma's words broke my heart.

I took her hands gently in mine, and opened them, so I could see her naked body. I looked at her from head to toe.

Emma was petite, but she didn't have the slim, firm figure like she had when she was 21. Her belly had a few unwanted pounds, and her hips and behind were thick.

Her breasts were small. They sagged a bit, probably from age and breastfeeding her 2 children. No one would call her tits perky. But her nipples were nice. They were like small erasers.

And her legs were still long and shapely. And her feet were small and pretty.

And her face was pretty too. Not youthful, not fresh-faced as it had been when she was 21. But pretty.

No one would call the 43-year-old Emma a hot MILF, or a hot cougar. But she wasn't bad. She was still fuckable.

And she used to babysit me. She used to be my babysitter! That by itself gave her a kinky element of hotness.

I found myself getting hard in my pants.

I took off my shirt and my pants. Emma looked at my young, muscular body for a long time. And then she caressed my young, muscular body for a long time.

"Mikey, god," Emma said with awe. "Your body is amazing."

Then I dropped my boxers and Emma looked at my cock for the first time. At this point I was completely hard. She stared at my thick, 10 inches.

Emma blushed and covered her mouth. "Oh my Mikey," Emma said, awe again in her voice. "You're so big."

I asked, "Is my cock bigger than your asshole ex-husband?"

Emma grinned at my question. Her smile lit up the room, and it was like she was a young girl again. "So much bigger, Mikey," she said. "William's so small compared to you."

I carried Emma to her bed. I got on top and kissed her lips and caressed her body. Emma hadn't forgotten how to kiss. She was a good kisser. I especially liked her soft tongue, and the way she urgently probed my mouth.

I went down on Emma. She screamed as I got her off. For a moment, I think she passed out. She later told me her husband had never eaten her pussy. She hadn't had a man's tongue lick her clit since she was my babysitter, when she had a brief fling with a college friend.

Then I fucked Emma. I'd like to say we made love, but I'm not a love making kind of guy.

I fucked Emma. It took her a while to get used to my size, and I went slow, but once I was in, I fucked her.

Emma's pussy wasn't the tightest I'd ever had, but it wasn't the loosest either.

Emma came twice while I fucked her, both times screaming and gripping my shoulders and back so hard she almost broke skin.

When I was close, Emma insisted I cum inside her. She said, "I can still have children – I think – but don't worry. I'll do Plan B tomorrow. I just want to feel a man cum inside me again."

I must admit, the idea of breeding my old babysitter got me super excited. When I came, I splashed her unprotected pussy with a ton of my seed. It was one of the best orgasms of my life.

EPILOGUE – *12 MONTHS Later*

EMMA HIRED ME. I'M doing well in her company. I'm now an account exec and have a good direction for my career.

I admit, part of my quick rise (I'm the youngest account exec in her company) is because I keep Emma's body happy. And it's no hardship on my part to fuck her a few times a week.

Emma dyed and styled her hair and is spending more time on her makeup. And, she's lost weight and firmed up her body by regular yoga and Pilates classes. And she still has those amazing legs.

Emma is dressing sexier, wearing short skirts, stockings and stiletto heels to show off those legs. Often, she goes braless, as she likes the horny looks she gets from men when her hard nipples dent her silky tops and dresses. Or when she "accidentally" flashes the lacy tops of the thigh high stockings she always wears now under her tight, short skirts.

Emma has turned into a hot MILF! Seriously! She is a hot cougar!

Our sexual relationship is a secret, of course. It wouldn't help either of us if people knew the CEO was fucking the young account exec. The benefit though, is I hear people talk. And I tell Emma what I hear. She loves hearing about the men in her company who want to fuck her.

Emma is still not on birth control. She's still completely unprotected. I told her about my breeding fantasy. She got hot when I admitted this to her, because the possibility that the boy she used to babysit gets her pregnant really turns her on.

I do pull out during her risky times of the month. But the risk is exciting for both of us.

Once she got her sexy body back, Emma called up her ex-husband Willaim, and they met for coffee. He went wild seeing this new Emma. He said if she looked this good back then, he wouldn't have cheated on her, and wouldn't have divorced her. At least William is consistent at being a dick.

Emma let William take her to his bed. She let him fuck her hot MILF body.

I got pissed. He was a dick to her! Why would she let him do that! And I was jealous too!

"It was a pity fuck, and William knew it," Emma said as she crawled on top of me and put my cock inside her. "I told him about you. How I'm fucking the boy I used to babysit. I told him you're way bigger, and you fuck me way better. I told him I feel sorry for his wife – he married one of those tramps he cheating with—because all she gets is his little dick."

"God you feel so good inside me!" Emma moaned as she rode my cock. "You feel so much better than William! His dick is so little, and he can't get as hard as you! You fuck me so much better! I *do* feel sorry for his wife!"

I laughed at her nasty talk. But I was still pissed. I told her to never again fuck another man without my permission.

Do we have a future together? I don't know. It's hot fucking a sexy MILF, and the fact she used to be my babysitter makes it extra hot. I actually think she's prettier and sexier now at 43, than when we first met when she was 21.

I do crave different pussy though. And younger pussy. I want Emma, but I want variety too.

I won't be a dick about it, like her ex William. I'll make sure Emma's body is taken care of. She fantasizes about getting gang banged.

I told her I'll set it up. It'll be easy.

Lots of guys my age would jump at the chance to fuck a sexy MILF like Emma.

BLACK SUPREMACY CUCKS HUSBAND TWICE

"I see you've done well for yourself," said Harry's ex-girlfriend Lise, eyeing Harry's pretty Chinese wife Mei.

Harry hadn't seen Lise in over 7 years. He married Mei 3 years ago. The 3 ran into each other in a Victoria's Secrets of all places.

They were talking in the bra section. Harry often went lingerie shopping with Mei, as she liked his opinion of what would look good on her.

"Nice to meet you," said Mei. She was an immigrant from Shanghai, China. She was fluent in English but had a sweet, soft Chinese accent. "You and Harry used to date, I think?"

"Yes, but that was years ago. We parted as friends, right Harry?" Lise said with a grin to her old boyfriend. Harry nodded but he avoided looking into Lise's eyes.

Harry's relationship with Lise had actually been painful for him. Even years later, he still had PTSD over that pain and how their relationship ended.

When Harry first began dating Mei, he told her about Lise and showed her pictures of his old girlfriend. Lise was very attractive – hot! – and Harry thought Mei would be impressed if she knew he had dated such a beautiful and sexy girl.

Harry told Mei that Lise had become interested in black men and that's why they broke up, but he didn't go into details. Harry had never told Mei the whole story about Lise and black men, and he hoped he never would have to.

The two women couldn't possibly be more different, although both were very pretty.

Lise was tall for a girl at 5'9". She had a classic hourglass figure with big breasts, curvy hips and a shapely bubble butt. Lise was a natural blonde and wore her hair past her shoulders.

Mei was the opposite. The pretty Chinese girl was 5'2". She had short black hair and slanty almond eyes. She was skinny and flat-chested. She had slim hips and her butt was almost as flat as her chest. From the neck down, Mei could almost be mistaken for a boy. Yet, there was something distinctly feminine and alluring about her, by the way she elegantly walked, the way she tilted her head when she was thinking about something, the way she played with her hair when she was talking to you. Also, Mei had amazing long, shapely legs.

Mei at 38 was older than Lise and Harry who were both 31, but like many Chinese girls, she had the face and body of a much younger girl. People looking at Mei would think she was in her early 20s.

Mei and Lise were also different in an important way. Lise didn't have any children. Mei though had a young son, Jiehong. Harry wasn't the father. The father was Mei's ex-boyfriend, a Chinese man. That relationship obviously didn't work out since Mei was Harry's wife. Harry was good with Jiehong and had actually adopted him as his son. He hoped to have his own child with Mei soon. Jiehong was a cute boy (just like his mother), and Harry really looked forward to seeing what their mixed white/Chinese child would look like.

⬦

"HONEY GUESS WHAT?" Mei said when Harry came home from work later that week. "Lise's taking me to some boutique clothes stores. She says she knows really good ones that aren't expensive."

Harry got a sinking feeling in the pit of his stomach. The last thing he wanted was for his wife to hang around with Lise. He didn't want Lise to rub off on Mei.

Before Mei, Harry used to only date white girls. He especially had a thing for blondes with big breasts and curvy bodies. That's why he fell so in love – and in lust – with Lise, because she was all that and more.

But after Harry's terrible experience with Lise, and his dating after their breakup (always white girls with big breasts and shapely bubble butts), he swore off ever dating another white girl again. That's when Harry switched to Chinese girls, and why he eventually dated and married Mei, a skinny, flat chested Asian girl with a tiny ass.

It had to do with the rising Black Supremacy movement that was all over the US. Most people incorrectly thought this was a political movement, and it was the same as Black Lives Matter. But Black Supremacy had nothing to do with Black Lives Matter.

Instead, Black Supremacy was about black men being sexually superior to white men. It was about black men being *REAL* men, and white men being boys in comparison. It was about black men having big black cocks (BBC) and white men having little boy dicks.

Black Supremacy was about black men dating white girls and making them *"Black Only."* It was about black men breeding their Black Only white girls, having chocolate babies, and eradicating white skin, blonde hair and blue eyes from the planet.

White fathers, husbands and boyfriends said blacks were trying to ruin their sweet white girls. That wasn't true at all. The black men in the Black Supremacy movement wanted to free white girls from the shackles forced upon them by small minded, inferior white men, and give those white girls the sexual pleasure and beautiful chocolate babies that they deserved.

Harry and Lise's relationship had been going well. They were in love and both content sexually. Harry was close to asking Lise to marry him.

But then Lise discovered Black Supremacy – and she experienced BBC. Soon after, Lise told Harry she believed in the Black Supremacy movement, and she was going to become a "Black Only" white girl.

Lise told Harry she wanted to stay with him, because she did love him. But because she was now "Black Only," she would no longer give him her pussy. In the Black Supremacy vernacular, Harry would become a "Pussy Free" white boy. But Lise promised to take care of his sexual needs with her hand and mouth. And she promised to be as loving as ever, except for a few nights a week when she would be with her black lovers.

Harry, as a proud white man, could not live under Lise's terms. Their breakup broke his heart. He liked to think Lise mourned the end of their relationship too, and maybe she did, but he heard through friends that she was spending a lot of her evenings with her black male friends – probably on her back in their beds—and becoming an advocate for the Black Supremacy Movement. And addicted to BBC.

Harry tried dating other white girls, but this happened over and over again. Harry would begin dating a pretty white girl, get serious with her, but then after a few months she would discover the Black Supremacy Movement. She would be tempted by a handsome, charismatic, well-endowed black men, and then after she experienced his BBC, she would either break up with Harry or give him an ultimatum like Lise had.

Harry tried to be reasonable with these white girls. He said he would agree to her being "Black Only," as long as she still gave him access to her pussy. Not always, just sometimes. But making white boys "Pussy Free" was a critical element of Black Supremacy. Black men did not want to mix their powerful seed with the far-inferior seed of weak, pathetic white men.

So finally, Harry made the decision to switch his love interests from white girls to Chinese girls. And not just any Chinese girls, but ones with little breasts and slim hips and behinds. He knew black men were attracted to curvy girls with big breasts and bubble butts. Harry thought by switching to a skinny, flat chested Chinese girl, he would no longer have to worry about the Black Supremacy Movement or competition from black men.

Mei came to the US from China for college. After getting her degree, she went back to China but found herself unattracted to Chinese boys – who she called "rice-boys." After experiencing the US and American culture during college, Mei found she was now attracted to white boys.

Mei did have a fling with a Chinese man and he got her pregnant. That relationship didn't last, but she decided to have the baby, a son, who she named Jiehong.

Mei moved back to the US and went to grad school. Then she got a job in the IT industry. She dated only white boys, but unfortunately, she never met the right man. Also, even though she was very pretty, many white men lost interest in her when they found out she had a son.

This all changed when Mei met Harry a few years ago. This was around the time he switched to Chinese girls. They met in a bar and Harry asked her on a date. Mei was thrilled Harry was interested in her, because he was white and had good career prospects. Also, Harry was a few years younger, and she thought it exciting for her, an older mom (a MILF) to date a younger white boy.

She was also thrilled when Harry didn't mind she had a son. Harry liked Jiehong. But the real reason he didn't mind, was he thought it was even less likely a black man would target Mei since she had a full-blood Chinese son (i.e., not a mixed Chinese / black son).

But then Harry and Mei ran into his ex-girlfriend, Lise, at Victoria's Secrets. And Lise invited Mei to hang out. The last thing Harry wanted was for Lise to tell his sweet Chinese wife about the Black Supremacy Movement and how it had ended their relationship.

———◉———

"WHAT'S THE MATTER?" Mei said one evening, when Harry was moping around.

"Nothing."

Mei could tell something was bothering her husband.

After a few glasses of wine, Harry started to open up.

"It's that girl, Lise," said Harry. "I don't like you hanging out with her."

"Why?" said Mei. "She's so nice to me. And she's taking me really interesting places, little fashion boutiques and interesting restaurants. Today, she took me to a Chinese restaurant and, gosh Harry, it was better than anything in Shanghai!"

Harry frowned. He didn't know his wife had been with Lise today. That made 4 times this week! She was socializing with Lise even more than he thought!

Harry decided he needed to level with Mei about Lise. He asked, "Do you remember why I broke up with her?"

"You mean, that thing about black men?"

Harry nodded.

"Oh, honey! You don't need to worry about me switching to black men! I love only you. Remember?" She gave her husband a kiss on the cheek.

"Other girls have told me that," Harry said with a sour look.

"Honey, I might look like a little girl, but remember, I'm almost 40," Mei said. "Even if black men *are* better, I'm done with all that. I'm settled down."

"I know...," Harry said with another frown, looking concerned. "But I don't want to be just the guy you *settled* for!"

"Stop worrying," Mei said. With a sly smile, she said, "I I know what will cheer you up."

Mei climbed on Harry's lap and started making out with him. Soon, clothes were coming off and forming a pile on the floor. Mei nibbled on Harry's chest and twirled the tip of her tongue around his nipples which she knew he loved. She sensually rubbed her little flat Chinese butt against his boxers.

"Harry, you know *this* is what I want!" Mei said as she reached between their bodies into her husband's boxers, and wrapped her hand around his hard cock. Mei was addicted to white men and white cock! She had sworn long ago to never touch another rice-boy cock.

Just like Lise was addicted to black cock and swore to never touch another whiteboy, Mei was addicted to white cock and swore to never again touch another rice-boy dick. And she honestly had never considered sex, and certainly not a relationship, with a black man.

Mei got on her knees and started deep-throating Harry's hard white penis, making cute little gagging noises.

"Oh Harry!" Mei said, wiping pre-cum off her lips. "You know I'm addicted to white-boy dick. I can't get enough of your white cock. I'm a white boy-only girl."

Mei's assurances (and her lips around his cock) made Harry feel better, but he was still uneasy about Mei spending so much time with Lise. Lise was an advocate for Black Supremacy. And one of the tenets of the movement was to get white girls to dump their white husbands for black men. If more white boys became "Pussy Free," then it would speed the eradication of white skin and the inferior white race.

Why was Lise spending so much time with Mei, if it wasn't her goal to hook Mei up with a black man, and to introduce her to BBC?

Mei rose up and reached for a condom. Harry was disappointed as she rolled the latex down his hard shaft. "Come on Mei, let's go bareback, just this time," Harry pleaded. "I'll pull out, I promise."

Mei shook her head. That was exactly what her ex-Chinese boyfriend had said, and she ended up getting pregnant. Since then, she had been anal about condoms. Mei was especially careful since she wasn't on any birth control. The pill screwed up with her hormones and always gave her terrible migraine headaches.

"Shhhhhhh," Mei said, touching Harry's lips with her finger. "You know I'm not on birth control." Then she stood up, rising up on her tiptoes and arching her back to pose sensually for her husband. "And you don't want me to go through pregnancy again, and risk losing my tight rice-girl body, do you?"

Harry moaned as he ran his eyes over his wife's slim, tight Chinese body. He used to crave big breasted woman with plump bubble butts, like Lise. But now after years with Mei, Harry desired only skinny Chinese girls like Mei. He even found his wife's little tits and flat butt to be big turn-ons!

Even though she was 38 years old, Mei's youthful, pretty Chinese face and her slim body made her look much younger, like a barely legal girl! Harry couldn't imagine going back to curvy white girls like Lise. Lise was still beautiful and sexy, but he no longer desired her. He wanted only skinny Chinese girls like Mei.

Mei lowered herself onto her husband, guiding his rubber-coated cock into her pussy. She moaned as she felt Harry's manhood through the rubber. That was something else Mei loved about white boys. Their cocks were so much bigger than rice-boy dicks!

⸺⸺◈⸺⸺

THE FIRST TIME MEI met her future black lover was in a Starbucks. She was there with (her new) best friend, Lise.

"Mei, this is Lamonte. Lamonte, Mei," Lise said.

"Nice to meet you." Mei shook Lamonte's hand.

Lamonte was Lise's favorite black lover. He was tall, well-built, and very fashionable. And his penis was the definition of BBC.

"The pleasure is all mine," Lamonte said, taking Mei's hand and kissing it. Mei was taken aback. No man had ever kissed her hand before. She was shocked but also charmed by the gesture.

As they spoke, Mei was impressed at how intelligent and well-spoken Lamonte was. Growing up in China, Mei had always been taught that black men were brute animals, barely any different than gorillas. "I guess I was wrong," she thought to herself.

Mei looked at Lamonte, like she was looking at a black man for the first time. Not only was he refined, but he was also very handsome, and so well dressed. Mei couldn't help feeling impressed by Lamonte, even enchanted.

———⬥———

"LAMONTE LIKES YOU," the text message from Lise said. Mei was checking her phone after getting home from the Starbucks.

Mei replied with a smiley face.

"Who are you texting?" Harry asked, coming up behind his wife.

"Just Lise," Mei said.

"I hope she's not a bad influence," Harry said looking concerned.

"Oh Harry-Bear, you worry too much," Mei said with a sweet smile. Mei's pet name for her husband was Harry-Bear. Harry's pet name for his wife was "Mei-Baby" (pronounced "My Baby").

But Mei realized Lise *was* a bad influence on her. She couldn't stop thinking about Lamonte after meeting him at Starbucks.

"Damn, Mei-baby, what's gotten into you?" Harry said later that night when Mei attacked him in the bedroom.

Mei was hornier than she'd been in a long time. She was practically throwing herself at her husband.

"Just showing my Harry-Bear some affection," Mei said as she kissed him open mouth. She pushed her tongue down Harry's throat, which is something she rarely did. Proper sweet Chinese girls like Mei did not tongue their men.

The married couple fell into their bed. They hurriedly undressed each other.

"Grrrr!" Mei growled playfully as she got on top of Harry, acting like a Chinese tiger. Despite her playfulness, her pussy was on fire. It was throbbing.

Harry didn't know it, but the reason his wife was so turned on was from meeting Lamonte earlier that day. The skinny rice-girl intended to pleasure her husband because she felt guilty for thinking about the black Lamonte so much. If she got pleasure in the process, though, there was nothing wrong with that.

Even as horny as she was, Mei still remembered the condom. She reached for one from the bedside cabinet, and rolled the latex down her husband's hard shaft.

"Harder! Harder!" Mei begged, stretching her long shapely legs over Harry's shoulders and urging him to fuck her harder. But something felt wrong tonight. It felt like something was missing, like sex with her husband was suddenly second-best.

"Oh god!!!!!" Harry cried. He couldn't last any longer. He orgasmed and ejaculated his sperm uselessly into the condom.

As she always did after sex, Mei wrapped her arms around her husband and snuggled him. As she kissed him, she said, "I love you, Harry-Bear."

"I love you too, Mei-Baby," Harry said feeling happy. He was sexually satisfied after such passionate sex and such an amazing orgasm. He felt so close to his wife. He realized his concerns about Lise were probably unfounded.

But Mei felt differently. While outwardly she was the same loyal rice-girl wife, inside she was unsatisfied. Harry had cum so fast, she didn't have a chance to reach her own orgasm. More than that, though, she could help thinking about Lise. Was her new BFF in bed right now with Lamonte? She knew Lise had gotten addicted to black men, and that's why she broke up with Harry. Was Lamonte one of Lise's black lovers? Were Lamonte and Lise having sex at that very moment?

After Harry fell asleep, Mei quietly rubbed herself. She tried not to think about Lamonte, but whenever her thoughts drifted to him, she got closer to an orgasm. Finally, Mei gave into it and fantasized about Lamonte fucking her little rice-girl body. Mei had to clench her teeth together to keep from screaming as she came really hard.

"HEY! MEI! REMEMBER me?"

It was Lamonte. Mei and Harry were at the local market and Lamonte just *happened* to run into them. Actually, it wasn't an accident. Lise had told Lamonte where the married couple shopped for groceries, and he had been staking out the place.

"Who is this, Mei?" Harry asked with a frown as he looked at the tall, muscular black man.

"This is Lamonte," Mei said. "He's Lise's friend. Lamonte, this is my husband, Harry!"

The white man and black man shook hands and made small-talk. Out of the corner of his eyes, Harry saw his wife staring at Lamonte's face and body, checking him out.

"We should be going Mei," Harry told his wife.

"Hey Mei, wanna grab lunch sometime? You wouldn't mine, right Harry?" Lamonte asked Mei.

Without waiting for Harry to answer, Lamonte handed his cell phone to Mei. "Here, call yourself and then we'll have each other's numbers," the black man said.

Mei looked at her husband for a moment, then she called herself using Lamonte's cell.

As soon as Lamonte was gone, Harry turned on his wife. "Why did you do that?" he demanded.

"I was just being nice," Mei said. "He's really good friends with Lise. So I can't exactly blow him off. That would be rude."

"But you know my issues!" Harry said with exasperation. "You know what happened with Lise!"

"Harry-Bear, you don't have to worry," Mei said reassuringly. She affectionately rubbed her husband's arm. "I'm not Lise. I'm your little rice-girl. And you're my big strong white-boy. You know only white-boys and white boy-dicks get me hot."

MEI'S PHONE DINGED. She suspected it would be Lamonte texting her. The two had been exchanging texts for a while now. Still, Mei's heart did a flip when she saw the text *was* from Lamonte.

She excused herself to the bathroom so she could look at Lamonte's text without Harry seeing.

Lamonte's texts had been getting more and more flirty. And sexual!

This one though was something new. Lamonte texted a picture of his penis!

Mei couldn't believe her eyes. Lamonte's cock was enormous! It had a huge fat head and thick veins running underneath and along the sides. "That big thing would destroy my little rice-girl body," she thought to herself.

Lamonte texted again. "Send me a picture of your pussy. I bet it's pretty."

Mei hesitated. Sending a picture of her most private part would be wrong! She was married! She would be betraying Harry!

But seeing Lamonte's big black cock had gotten Mei so hot. She pulled down her pants and panties and took a picture of her pussy.

Mei had thick black pubic hair. She was embarrassed for Lamonte to see her unruly bush, as she knew girls nowadays trimmed or got Brazilians. She wished she had time to trim her bush, but Harry was outside, and he would suspect something if she stayed in the bathroom too long.

Mei felt guilty she wanted to be clean shaven for Lamonte, but she didn't feel that way for her husband.

With an inward shrug, Mei took a picture of her hairy pussy and texted it to Lamonte.

———●———

THE NEXT DAY LISE TEXTED. "Hey bad girl, heard you're sexting with Lamonte."

"Yeah," Mei answered. She had deleted the picture of Lamonte's cock – a faithful wife should not have such pictures on her phone. But just thinking about Lamonte's huge manhood made Mei tingle between her legs.

"Please don't tell Harry."

"I've got Go-Go lips," Lise texted, referring to the girl band's song, *My Lips Are Sealed*. "Do you want me to hook you up?"

"I can't," Mei answered. "Harry would die if I had sex with a black man. You know how he is."

"Forget that micro-dick loser," Lise texted.

"Please don't say that about my husband," Mei said. "I know you two didn't work out, but I'm not you. I love Harry."

"I loved the white boy too, back then," Lise said. "I would have stayed with him. Maybe even married him. But he wouldn't agree to the Black Supremacy rules."

Mei stared at Lise's text, not understanding. "What?"

"You don't know about Black Supremacy?"

"No."

Lise gleefully texted a link of the Black Supremacy website to Mei. Mei's eyes grew wide as she followed the link and read what was there. And the tingling in her pussy grew stronger.

———◉———

LAMONTE BEGAN TEXTING Black Supremacy propaganda to Mei. Almost hourly, Mei would get a picture of a pretty girl sucking a huge black cock. Or a tiny skinny girl impaled on a BBC. The pictures had captions, like "Upgrade from TINY white dick to BIG black cock" or "Cheat on your WEAK husband with a POWERFUL black man today."

What surprised Mei was all the girls in the pictures were Chinese, not white. She thought black men chased after busty white girls, not skinny Chinese rice-girls like her.

The pictures aroused Mei – especially since the Chinese girls in the pictures all looked like her (pretty, thin, black hair to just below her ears, flat chested, shapely legs) but they made her feel guilty too. She felt like she was betraying Harry, especially with his long bad history of losing girlfriends to black men.

After about a week of the photos, Mei texted to Lamonte, "Please stop. This isn't right. I'm married to a white man. This is disrespecting him."

What Mei didn't know, though, was Lamonte *wanted* to disrespect Harry. His goal was to poison Mei's relationship with her husband. Lamonte didn't want to destroy her marriage – the Black Supremacy movement needed white money to survive and thrive, so they wanted Black Only white wives to stay with their Pussy Free white husbands.

Lamonte wanted to destroy Mei and Harry's *sexual* relationship. The black man wanted Mei to lose respect for Harry in bed, and to lose all sexual desire for her husband's weak white body and little white pencil dick.

Lamonte upped the game by sexting videos to Mei. The videos were of black men fucking pretty Chinese girls. Like the photos, the Chinese girls in all the videos closely resembled her.

Mei had resisted masturbating to the photos, but with the videos she couldn't resist. The videos weren't professional, from a film studio. Instead, they were homemade and amateur, which made them much more authentic – and hot!

The videos showed big black cocks *DESTROYING* tiny little rice-girl pussies like hers, and they turned her on so much! When Harry was at work, Mei spent time in bed, naked, watching the videos as she played with herself. She always came so hard looking at the videos.

AFTER LAMONTE HAD BEEN sexting Black Supremacy videos to Mei for a couple weeks, she asked Lise to meet her for lunch. "You've got to get Lamonte to stop texting me pictures and videos!" the pretty little Chinese girl begged. "It's driving me crazy!"

"Crazy like you're finally ready to try out Lamonte's beautiful black body and big black cock?" Lise asked with a grin.

"Lise, you know I can't do that!" Mei said pleadingly. "I've never cheated on Harry! And even if I did, it couldn't be with a black man! It would kill Harry!"

Lise didn't argue. She ordered a bottle of wine and poured vino down Mei's throat until she was tipsy and her inhibitions were down. Lise knew Mei wanted desperately to fuck Lamonte. She had been there! Lise knew she only needed to nudge the Chinese girl a little.

"I want to treat you to something," Lise said, curling her arm in Mei's and leading her to a salon down the street. Once inside one of the treatment rooms, she told Mei to undress. "Lamonte showed me the picture of your pussy. Girlfriend, you need to shave all that ugly pubic hair off."

Mei hesitated. Even though she was half-drunk, she could sense a trap.

Seeing her hesitation, Lise said, "Tonight you'll go home and show Harry your bare pussy and he'll go crazy. You're probably feeling guilty about Lamonte. Am I right? I know I'm right, I've been there, girlfriend. So let me pay to get you a Brazilian, and then you can let Harry go wild with your body tonight."

Mei hesitated a moment longer, then she nodded and took off her clothes. Lise was right. This was a good way of making things right with her husband.

The therapist came into the room and Brazilian'ed Mei's pussy and ass. She also waxed Mei's long, shapely legs. When the therapist was done, the only hair Mei had left were on her pretty rice-girl head.

The therapist left the room and Mei was about to get up to dress, but then Lise was standing at the end of the table she was laying on. "Lise, what?" Mei said, surprised to see her.

"You need this moisturizer, or you might get a rash," Lise said softly. Lise squirted a clear liquid from a bottle onto her fingers, and then gently rubbed where Mei used to have pubic hair. Her pussy, the crack between her cheeks, around her puckered asshole.

Mei immediately felt the soothing effect of the moisturizer. "Thank you, Lise," she said.

"I'm not done, Mei-baby" Lise said, using Harry's pet name for his wife. Her fingers went from soothing to caressing. Lise was touching Mei's pussy, her clit, her sandbar, her ass, in a sensual way, not the clinical way the therapist had touched her.

Mei couldn't help getting turned on. She wasn't into girls – she wasn't bi curious at all—but her body was responding to Lise's caresses. She couldn't help moaning, her nipples got hard, and her body squirmed as Lise worked on her.

"I think you're ready, Mei," Lise said. She poured more of the clear liquid on the rice-girl's pussy lips and caressed the moisturizer – it was really a lubricant – around and into Mei's pussy.

Mei moaned as Lise pushed 2 fingers into her, to make her pussy slick and wet. "What do you mean, I'm ready?" she gasped. Mei now was panting from arousal. "Ready for what?"

And then, suddenly, it wasn't Lise standing there. She moved to the side, and someone else took her place.

It was Lamonte! And he was completely naked!

Mei stared at Lamonte. His body was so muscular, so well-defined! He was so handsome too, gorgeous! And his cock was hard and so big, it was almost the size of her forearm!

And Lamonte's skin was jet black!

"You have to ask me, Mei," Lamonte said as he pressed the fat head of his cock against Mei's pussy lips. "Black men don't rape girls. You have to ask me."

"I'm married, Lamonte," Mei said desperately.

Lamonte pressed slightly harder against Mei's pussy lips with his cock. "Do you really care about him now, Mei?"

Yes, Mei *did* care about Harry. She took her marriage vows seriously.

But after all the flirting with Lamonte, all the pictures and videos, all the masturbating while fantasizing about Lamonte – and after Lise worked her body to a frenzy – Mei could no longer resist.

She needed to experience Lamonte! She needed to experience black cock!

Mei finally said, "I want you Lamonte."

Lamonte grinned, flashing perfect, brilliant white teeth. Then he pushed forward. He penetrated Mei's married pussy.

Mei groaned at the sudden thickness inside her. But Lamonte knew how to get wives like Mei accustomed to his size. He went slow, taking his time. Eventually his big, thick cock was inside Mei's tiny little rice-girl pussy.

Lamonte didn't try to go balls deep into Mei. Not this first time with her, and not the next either. That would come later. She needed to be stretched first. But the black man knew he *would* stretch Mei's tight rice-girl pussy until it fit his cock like a glove. And the fact her pussy would then be *ruined* for her husband's little white boy dick made it all the better.

———◉———

EPILOGUE

———◉———

MEI DIDN'T LIE TO HARRY. She told him about her affair with Lamonte.

Mei tried to be loyal to her husband, she tried to make her hook-up with Lamonte a one-time thing. But in the end, she couldn't resist Lamonte. And she couldn't resist the other gorgeous, powerful, well-hung black men Lise introduced her too. As they say, once a girl goes black, she doesn't go back. That's what happened to Mei.

It was like Lise all over again. Mei told Harry she was now Black Only. She didn't want a divorce, she still loved him, but now more in a platonic, best friend kind of way.

But to stay married to her, Harry had to agree to become Pussy Free. He could still see Mei naked, kiss her, and touch her. And Mei would make him cum with her mouth and hands. But he would never again be allowed in her pussy.

Before, Harry broke up with Lise when she gave him this ultimatum. This time, though, he agreed. He surrendered to Black Supremacy.

Harry felt he had to. Lise had been just his girlfriend. Mei was his *wife*. And he had adopted her son, Jiehong, and he loved the boy. He couldn't imagine a life without Mei and Jiehong.

So, Harry agreed. He became a Pussy Free husband. For the second time in his life, black men had cuckolded him.

It wasn't easy for Harry, because at least once a week, and often more, Mei spent the night with one of her black boyfriends. While Harry took care of Jiehong, his wife was giving her tight, skinny rice-girl body to black men.

About half the time, Mei's black boyfriends fucked her at their house. Harry was allowed to watch. The black men *wanted* Pussy Free white husbands to watch as they fucked their Black Only wives, to see how inadequate and weak they were compared to black men.

To his surprise, Harry found himself aroused watching Mei getting fucked by her black boyfriends. It shamed him and he hated himself as he jerked off watching his wife getting fucked. But he couldn't resist and he always had explosive orgasms.

Never again, though, would his sperm be ejaculated into Mei's pussy. He was a Pussy Free white husband, after all. Harry's dream of having a baby with his wife was gone.

Mei did have more children though. It was an important principle of Black Supremacy that black men breed their Black Only wives. Mei was bred twice by black men, and had two beautiful, exotic looking black/Chinese mixed girls. Harry was a good man, so he adopted both girls even though it was clear to everyone he was not the biological father.

About a year after Mei gave birth to the second girl, she let Harry make love to her. Her black boyfriends gave her permission to do so. It wasn't to be kind to the cuckold husband. Instead, it was to show Harry how they had ruined his wife's pussy for his little white boy dick.

When Harry pushed his hard dick into Mei, he went in balls deep with hardly any resistance. His wife's pussy, which used to be tight and snug around his just over 5-inch cock, was so loose he could barely feel anything.

When Harry realized that – when he realized the black men *had* ruined his wife's pussy for his white boy cock – he started to cry. He knew then that even if Mei someday stopped being Black Only and returned to being his faithful wife, neither of them would ever enjoy sex with each other ever again.

HOMELESS BLACK MAN FUCKS UNPROTECTED WIFE IN ALLEY

My wife and I play games. We like to pretend she's getting fucked by other men.

It's just a game. We're not swingers. We would never bring another man into our marriage for real. But *pretending* she's with another man always gets us both hot.

To make it more real, I bought a cock sleeve. It's like a dildo, but it has a hole that I put my hard dick into. The cock sleeve makes my penis longer and thicker. So when I fuck my wife, it feels to her like it's a different cock inside her.

I have a few cock sleeves, actually. They vary in length and girth, but they are all bigger than my cock. I never tell Lacy – that's my wife's name – which I'm wearing, so that makes our fantasy of her with another man feel even more real.

When we're playing the game, Lacy says nasty things, like "You're so much bigger than my husband!" and "You fuck me so much better than my husband!" I love it!

I'll say something like, "I bet you cheat on your husband all the time!"

And my wife will say, "Oh god yes! His dick is tiny! He never makes me cum! My loser husband can't make me cum with his little dick!"

Nasty talk like that gets us both off. I have cuckold fantasies so the idea of Lacy with a well-hung man gets me hot beyond belief. And, to be honest, my dick *is* small. It's just shy of 5 inches and thin.

Lacy didn't like it at first, but over the years my cuckold fantasies grew on her. Now she gets as turned on as me when we play our game.

We call it our C-Game. Our cuckolding game. The game where my Lacy – the love of my life – cucks me.

Sometimes we go to a bar – separately – and I watch as she flirts and dances with other men. This is one of our favorite C-Games and we do it all the time.

Lately we've gotten into the idea of Lacy with black men. So, I bought some black cock sleeves. Bigger than all the other cock sleeves. So Lacy can imagine she's with a Big Black Cock.

The idea of being with a black man is extra hot for Lacy. Extra taboo. But we'll get to that.

We've started going to bars that cater to black men who crave white pussy. It surprised us how many there are. You can find them yourself. Just Google "bars that cater to black men who crave white pussy."

It's more dangerous going to these bars, as black men are naturally more aggressive than white men, especially at these bars that they consider their home turf.

A few times, black men have seriously fondled Lacy's body and even gotten fingers up her dress and into her panties, usually while sucking face with my wife. So far we've been able to get out of those bars with Lacy's faithfulness still intact, and the evening always ends with great sex, me fucking Lacy with a black cock sleeve, pretending I'm the black man she traded spit with that night.

But like I said, this is all make believe, just a game. I never want, and Lacy never wants, to let another man inside her pussy. We're happily married, and even though my endowment isn't the biggest, our sex life is exciting and fulfilling.

We like to mix up our C-Game with different scenarios, to keep it fresh and exciting. To give you a more complete picture, I should tell you more about us. I'm 45 – my name is Mitch – and Lacy is 43. We've been married for 20 years.

Lacy told me early in our relationship that she didn't want any children. My wife – to be honest – is selfish and vain – I love her but it's true. She cares about her looks. It's important to her. *Very* important.

Lacy doesn't want childbirth and the emotional and physical stress of raising children to ravage her body or her face, which are both magnificent.

Even at 43, my wife is a hottie and a serious head-turner. She's tall with big natural perky tits, toned arms, sexy back, tight tummy, shapely yet firm ass and hips, toned thighs, long shapely legs, and tiny, pretty feet. Lacy's face is beautiful with long, wavy natural blonde hair.

Lacy's face and body are perfect. She's 43 but you could mistake her for 23. She's a godness. A ripe, sex goddess.

I was perfectly okay when she told me she didn't want kids. Even though we fantasize about cucking and cheating on me, she is completely faithful, so I'm the only man who gets the benefit of her beauty and sexiness. In fact, a few years ago, I got a vasectomy, so we would never again have to worry about her getting pregnant and losing her looks or tight, sexy body.

A few months ago, we went to a black bar and as we got out of the taxi, I saw a homeless bum sitting on the ground in an alley. The alley was next to the bar, and I had sudden inspiration to make our C-Game really exciting tonight.

Holding my wife's hand, I walked up to the bum. God he was disgusting. Old, dirty and he reeked of urine, cigarettes and cheap booze. His baggy clothes were ragged and filthy.

And the bum was black. I felt my wife stiffen when we approached, and she saw he was black.

My wife grew up in Mississippi, and while she was not overtly prejudiced, she didn't feel comfortable around black people, and intentionally didn't have any black friends. She was a conservative Republican and felt white people were better than black people. The last thing she wanted to do was talk to this filthy, black bum.

I held her hand tight and forced her to stand with me as I chatted with the black homeless man. He said everyone called him Nut because he liked peanuts. He said he was 50-something – he didn't know his exact age. He said he had been homeless for years, but he didn't know exactly how long. He said he spent most nights sleeping in this alley.

Nut said he knew the bar's reputation, about white girls (often married) going to this bar to have exciting flings with handsome, well-hung black men. Nut liked looking at these pretty white girls as they went in the bar in their short skirts and high heels; that's why he spent most evenings in this alley. He thought white girls, especially blonde, white girls, were the prettiest girls on the planet.

As he said this, Nut was leering at Lacy. Lacy *was* a blonde white girl. She was very pretty, a knockout. And whenever we played the C-Game, like tonight, she dressed to impress with a body hugging, short dress with a plunging neckline. Lacy didn't wear anything under the dress – it added to our fantasy that she was looking to get picked up to cheat on me— except for black thigh high stockings and 4-inch stiletto *fuck-me* high heels. Nut leered at my wife the entire time we were talking.

I gave Nut some money and then Lacy and I walked away.

"Mitch, why did you talk to that disgusting black man?" Lacy demanded. At this point, we were standing at the door to the bar.

I grinned and said, "I think Nut is going to fuck you tonight."

"What?" Lacy said, not understanding.

"You don't like black people, right?" I said. "How hot would it be if a filthy old black bum fucked you?"

Lacy's eyes got big as she caught up with my thinking. "Oh—my ...," she gasped. "You mean, in the alley?"

I was good at imitating people's voices, like movie stars. It made me popular at parties!

In Nut's voice, I said, "You want Nut's big black cock in your married pussy, slut?"

Lacy shuddered at my imitation of the filthy old homeless black man.

I grinned and said, "We're going to do this, in the alley, with Nut watching."

"Oh – my – god," Lacy moaned. She looked totally aroused. We had often pillow talked about playing our game in public spaces, with people watching. Tonight would be the first time we had done it for real. In public.

"Do you have – you know?" Lacy asked me.

I opened a bag I was carrying. Inside was a black cock sleeve. Hey, what can I say? I used to be a boy scout, so I'm always prepared!

Like always, Lacy went into the bar alone. I waited for about 10 minutes, and then I followed her.

As we usually did, Lacy and I sat at opposite ends of the bar, so I could watch her flirt with men. She was quickly surrounded by black men. After all, they were here for white girl pussy, and my wife (as usual) was easily the prettyish and sexiest woman in the room. And the fact the diamonds of her wedding and engagement rings were sparklingly made her even more desirable. Black men wanted *married* white pussy. They wanted to get married white women to cheat on their pathetic white husbands.

I could tell, though, that Lacy wasn't interested in any of the black men in the bar. Our C-Game tonight was going to be in the alley. So after about an hour and a half, she excused herself.

Lacy freshened herself in the lady's room. Then I watched as she navigated the crowded bar to the side door that led to the alley. She was shaking in her high heels, because she drank 4 strong appletinis (bought by black men) in the last 90 minutes. Lacy always drank a lot when we played our C-Game. It made it more real that she was cheating on her husband with another man if she was drunk.

I followed Lacy after about a minute. I didn't want her to be alone in the alley for too long, because Nut was there. Although I felt the black homeless man was harmless, because he was old, feeble, probably senile, and drunk himself.

It took me a while to get to the side door. The black men in this bar didn't appreciate a white man being there. I got a lot of shit from more than a few of these black men. When I finally made it to the side door, Lacy had been alone in the alley for about 20 minutes. Alone with Nut. Again, I wasn't worried, Nut was harmless.

But when I stepped into the alley, I found out I was wrong. Nut was anything *but* harmless.

Lacy was bent at the waist over a trash can. Her skirt was up around her waist.

The homeless black man, Nut, was behind her. His black cock was inside her. Nut was fucking my wife!

"So good!" Lacy moaned as Nut moved his cock in and out of my wife. "So fucking good!"

"Yeah, bitch, you getting Nut cock, you getting Nut cock good," Nut said as he fucked my wife.

I couldn't tell if Lacy knew it was Nut, or me fucking her. I found out a moment later, when Lacy giggled and said, "Mitch, *god*, you're playing the game so good, you even smell like Nut. How did you do that? Go in the bathroom and pee on yourself?"

Now I knew Lacy thought it was me fucking her from behind. And I saw Nut had his dirty black hand wrapped in Lacy's soft blonde hair, pressing her beautiful face against the top of the trash can, so she couldn't see behind her to see it wasn't me.

Lacy moaned as Nut penetrated her married white pussy with more of his cock. I saw his cock was huge! It must have been 11 inches, and as thick as Lacy's wrist! It was truly a *BIG BLACK COCK*!

"Mmm, that's right," Nut said approvingly. "Moan for Nut, bitch. Moan for Nut's big dirty cock."

Nut grunted from behind, his dirty fingernails digging into the firm, lily white skin of my wife's thighs. "Nut knew you be a good fuck. You like my nigger cock, bitch?"

Lacy moaned. She said, "That's so bad, Mitch, using the N-word! But so sexy, too!"

"Stop talking about Mitch, bitch!" Nut growled. "Who that? Your whitey husband? He got a little white boy dick, right? You with a real man now!"

"Oh god yes!" Lacy hissed as Nut began fucking her deeper and harder. "My husband has a little dick! You're so much bigger! You're a *man*, Nut! My husband is just a pathetic white *boy*!"

I should've stopped this. Run to Lacy's rescue.

But my cuckold fantasies took me over! For years we fantasized about me watching Lacy with other men! Now it was happening! It was happening, for real! I *wanted* it to happen!

Instead of ripping the filthy old black man from my wife, I took out my cock and started jerking off. I jerked off as I watched that filthy old black man fuck my wife!

"What yo name, slut?" Nut asked.

"Lacy," Lacy said. "I'm *your* Lacy, Nut! Not my husband's! I'm yours!"

Nut laughed. He fucked her even harder, and said, "That right. Daddy Nut gonna fuck yo pretty white pussy with my dirty nigger cock. Fuck you good until Nut gets his nut." Nut laughed again at his unintended joke.

"Say Nut name, Lacy. Say Nut. Tell Nut how much you want my nigger cock."

Mitch stepped closer until he was just a few feet away. Lacy's beautiful face was contorted in unmeasurable pleasure. Their mating looked so raw and animalistic. Jealously tore at his heart at never having seen her look this way with him.

"Nut," Lacy whimpered. "Oh, fuck, Nut. You fuck me so good Nut. So much better than my husband. I love your cock, Nut. I love your nigger cock. God Nut, I love you!"

Despite growing up in Mississippi, I had never heard Lacy say the N-word before. But the terrible word must have been deeply rooted in her psyche, as it sounded like a moan as she said it.

Hearing my beautiful white wife say his name, Nut launched into overdrive, fucking Lacy's pussy even harder and faster. Nut reached under her and roughly groped her breasts. My wife's breasts were magnificent, big yet still perky since they had never gone through the rigors and abuse of childbirth and breast feeding.

Lacy was fucking Nut back, thrusting her tight shapely ass back as he pushed forward into her. Nut was fucking my wife so hard, each of his powerful, forward thrusts pushed her stockinged feet out of the 4-inch stiletto high heels and onto her pretty, manicured tiptoes.

I saw the telltale signs of a man working himself up to a monumental orgasm, as Nut was clenching his hairy asscheeks, and his ball sack was tightening up.

I suddenly remembered Lacy wasn't on the pill! She was completely unprotected, and she was going to let Nut cum inside her because she thought it was me! Lacy didn't want to get pregnant because she wanted to keep her perfect face and body exactly the way they were, and she knew my sperm was useless because I got a vasectomy years ago.

I saw Lacy was close to an orgasm, too. I knew my wife, we had been married for 20 years, so I knew the signs, she was close to an intense orgasm. She confirmed it when she gasped, "Oh god, Nut, Nut, I'm close, you're going to make me cum, I'm cumming, I'm almost there ...."

Nut picked up his speed, desperate to cum in the sexy, beautiful married white wife, who was still bent at the waist with her pretty face still smashed against the top of the filthy garbage can. Nut felt her pussy gripping his black cock, wanting to milk out every last drop of his sperm.

Nut bared his teeth like a wild animal. A low grumbling began deep down in his throat that made him sound like a mangy hound about to strike its prey. His head shook violently, his cock feeling so good in the tight pussy of this sexy white wife, his orgasm so close.

Nut groped my wife's perfect, firm, heaving breasts again, pinching her nipples, and Lucy howled a loud moan. I had never heard my wife make these sounds before!

"Nut cumming, bitch!" Nut snarled. "Take it, bitch! Take my nigger cock! Take my nigger seed!"

Again, Nut using the N-word turned Lacy on even more. She became wild, delirious! I had never seen my wife like this, it was like she was a mad woman!

Lacy screamed, "Cum in me, Nut! I'm not protected, did you know that? Cum in my cheating, married, unprotected pussy! Shoot your nigger sperm into me! Bred me, Nut! Make me have your nigger baby! Make my belly fat! Make my ass and thighs thick! Make my tits sag! Ruin my perfect body! Make my husband cry when he sees my ruined body!"

I had never heard Lacy say such nasty, self-demeaning things. Did she fantasize about being bred and losing her looks? Was that one of her deep, dark secrets? Men using her body, breeding her, making her lose her perfect face and body?

I didn't have time to think about it as both Nut and Lacy came at the same time. They both screamed as their climaxes slammed down like a tidal wave slamming onto the beach.

Nut violently rammed my wife's pussy over and over, each time pumping jets of his black sperm into her.

It was at that moment that Lacy sensed something was wrong. The cock sleeves I used were like condoms. When I was wearing one, she never felt my sperm hitting her walls, because my spunk stayed inside the cock sleeve. It didn't matter either way, because I had had a vasectomy, but the point was, Lacy knew something was different this time. This time, she *did* feel powerful jets of sperm slamming her insides.

Lacy turned her head and looked over her shoulder. He eyes went wide with shock as she saw it wasn't me fucking her. It was that old, filthy, disgusting black homeless man, the real Nut.

And then Lacy saw me, standing a couple of feet away, my hand around my softening cock. My hand was wet from my own spunk, as I had cum when Nut impregnated – when Nut bred – my wife.

Then we heard applause. Both Lacy and I looked around. The black men she had flirted with in the bar were in the alley. They had seen it all, and now they were applauding.

The black men moved towards my wife. I tried to stop them, but they put me in an unbreakable neck hold. I couldn't move. I couldn't help my wife. All I could do was watch.

The black men – there were 4 of them – fucked my wife, one after another. She didn't try to stop them. She was defeated by this point.

The black men all fucked my wife bareback, and they all came inside her, adding their black seed to Nut's.

And while she was getting gang-banged by big black cock, she was screaming, and her beautiful face was wildly contorted. Not from pain or anguish, though. From lust. From indescribable pleasure. The black men were making my wife cum repeatedly on their big black cocks. It was the best fucking of her life. She had never cum so much, or so good.

———◉———

EPILOGUE – FIVE YEARS Later

———◉———

THAT NIGHT IN THE ALLEY changed our lives. Our C-Game went from fantasy to real. Lacy began fucking men for real, while I watched. We never used cock sleeves again. There was no need, as Lacy got all the big cocks she desired.

Lacy become hooked on black cock. She lusted for black men. She loved how they looked, how they smelled, how they kissed, how they talked, how they moved. My wife became addicted to black men.

And she lusted for their cocks. Their *Big Black Cocks.*

Lacy loved feeling those cocks inside her. She loved how those black men with their powerful black bodies and their long and thick black cocks literally destroyed her pussy. She loved it! And those black men always made her cum so hard.

Lacy rarely hooked up with just one black man. She wanted two or three black men at the same time, taking turns with her body, with her mouth, her pussy, and her ass. Or having them all inside her *at the same time*! She loved getting gang banged by black men.

Lacy has been bred twice in the last 5 years. She doesn't know who the fathers are. She only knows they are black. Because mine is the only white dick she ever lets inside her, and my sperm is useless since getting the vasectomy. And anyway, it's clear to anyone who looks that the fathers are black men, because the babies she gave birth to are clearly black.

Five years after what happened in the alley, Lacy's beautiful face is no longer flawless. The strain and rigors of giving birth and raising two very active half-black sons have caused wrinkles along her forehead, around her eyes, and the corners of her mouth.

And Lacy's body is no longer perfect. She tried her best to get her body back after each pregnancy, but it's hard for a 43-year-old woman to lose that much baby weight and to firm back up. Even harder for a 48-year-old woman, which she is now.

Lacy cries sometimes when she looks at her body in the full-length mirror. Her body is no longer perfect. She no longer has a flat tummy. She's gained weight around her hips. Her formerly tight ass now wiggles with fat. She has cellulite on the back of her thighs. Her big breasts sag because black men insist that their white mamas breast feed their black offspring.

Lacy is still attractive, she's still sexy. Her face and body are no longer perfect. But she is still fuckable. My wife is a MILF now.

And Lacy still gets all the black cock she wants. It turns out, black men prefer their white bitches to have big asses. And even though Lacy's breasts sag now, they got bigger from the two pregnancies, and black men like those big fleshy white tits.

Lacy still gives me her pussy whenever I want. She doesn't deny me, the way some white wives do to their white husbands after they go black.

But Lacy's pussy doesn't give me pleasure like before. Too much BBC and the pregnancies have stretched out her pussy. It's still pleasurable for black men and their big cocks, but for my average white dick, it feels loose. I can barely feel anything when I'm inside my wife.

But that's okay. It still gets me hot when I watch my wife with other men. I've learned to use Vaseline to grease up my cock when I watch. That way, I can slowly circle jerk and edge myself, so I don't cum too fast. I try to time my orgasms for when Lacy's black lovers climax and ejaculate their sperm into her.

Lacy is still not on any birth control. Her black lovers won't allow it. They want to breed my wife again. They figure they can breed her a couple more times before she gets too old.

At this point, Lacy *wants* to be bred again, she *wants* to carry a black man's baby again, no matter how another pregnancy will certainly further age her face, and further ruin her body. Because Lacy loves how it feels to get fucked by a black man when she's pregnant with a black baby. To Lacy, those are the best fucks.

To my wife, those are the fucks she craves the most.

BONUS SNEAK PEEK - DESIRING ANOTHER MAN'S WIFE

I felt nervous, this being our first function at the club. My wife Maddie and I didn't fit into this crowd of ultra-rich people. We joined this exclusive country club about a month ago so I could get to know people like this, to help me at work.

Maddie looked as nervous as me. Not only were we poor compared to all these rich people, but also much younger. I was 29 and Maddie 26, while everyone else was at least 15 years older.

I chatted with a distinguished black man who introduced himself as Victor. As we spoke, my attention was drawn to a beautiful woman standing across the room. She was tall with long dark hair and wore an elegant off-the-shoulder cocktail dress that ended about mid-thigh.

Unlike my blonde wife Maddie, who's petite and small breasted, this woman had a classic hourglass figure, with large breasts and curvy hips. Her legs weren't slim like Maddie's, but they were shapely and looked great in her stiletto high heels.

The woman eased herself into a seat at the bar. She ordered a drink, and as she did she crossed her legs. This made her dress hike up her thighs, but she quickly adjusted and pulled her dress back down her legs.

My eyes grew wide. For an instant, just before the woman pulled her dress down, her stocking tops were exposed, the dark welts of the sheer nude nylons straining against the straps of her black garter belt.

I've never known a woman who wore real stockings, the kind that's held up with a garter belt. I've seen them often enough in adult movies or on the internet, but I've never met a woman who wore them in public, in real life. I've encouraged Maddie to wear them, but in our entire relationship she's worn them only once, on our wedding day. Usually she goes without hose, or wears pantyhose, like tonight.

I felt myself stiffening, my full attention drawn to the woman. She looked to be Latino, with a dark exotic complexion. Her lips were full and painted bright red, and her large breasts almost spilled over the top of her strapless dress. My eyes focused on her legs. I hoped she'd cross her legs again, so I could glimpse her stocking tops again.

Victor saw my distraction and followed my eyes to the sensual woman. He smiled knowingly and gestured to the woman. The woman looked at Victor, and then at me. She smiled. She slipped off the chair, and once again I glimpsed a hint of her stocking tops. Then she began walking towards us. The ballroom was loud, but I imagined hearing the click-click of her high heels as she elegantly walked across the hardwood floor towards us.

I panicked. Victor had caught me ogling this sensuous woman, and now he was going to embarrass me in front of everyone. I looked around for Maddie, and found her just a few feet away, speaking to another couple. I hoped her conversation would continue while I dealt with this situation.

The woman arrived and stood in front of us, an almost teasing smile on her full painted lips. In her high heels she was taller than me but came to just Victor's chest.

"Sofia," Victor said, gesturing to me. "I'd like you to meet Adam."

Then Victor looked at me. "Adam, this is Sofia, my wife."

His wife?! My cheeks flushed red in embarrassment. "Hi, ah, nice to meet you," I managed to say as I extended my hand.

Sofia took my hand in hers, her touch light. "The pleasure is mine," she said as she looked into my eyes. Then, just before releasing my hand, she dug her long red nails into my palm. Sparks ran up my spine, and I gratefully grabbed a glass of wine from a passing waiter.

Sofia looked questioning behind me. "Where's your lovely wife? Madison, isn't it?"

"That's right," I said, surprised. How did she know my wife's name? But then I remembered the club emailed a newsletter listing all the new members, with our pictures. I turned and gestured to Maddie. "Honey, this is Victor and Sofia."

Maddie shook their hands, and we chatted about ourselves, while they entertained us with gossip about the club and its members. Victor and Sofia made a physically striking couple. He looked like he stepped out of *GQ*, and she *Vogue* magazine.

The cover band played a popular song, and Sofia took my hand. "Maddie, you don't mind if I dance with your husband, do you?"

Maddie looked a little tipsy, having had more than her share of wine. "Not at all," she said with a friendly lopsided smile.

"No need to worry," Victor said to me as he waved us away. "I'll keep your wife company."

I led Sofia onto the crowded dance floor. Feeling awkward, I took Sofia's hand in mine. Then, I hesitantly placed my other hand on her hip, making sure to stay well above the swell of her shapely ass.

Sofia smiled and we began to dance. She was an excellent dancer, sensually swaying to the music. The silky, barely-there material of her dress left little to the imagination, and I quickly realized she wasn't wearing a bra. I also felt the outline of her garter belt around her waist, and the effect on me (and my manhood) was what you'd expect.

The growing crowd pressed us together. I was embarrassed; certain Sofia could feel my erection pressing against her stomach. But she didn't pull away. If anything, Sofia pressed closer against me. I looked down, seeing the swells of her large breasts. Her hard, braless nipples caused dents in the filmy material of her dress. Sofia saw me looking down her dress. She looked into my eyes and smiled invitingly.

The dance ended, and I let Sofia go. Not because I wanted to, but because I didn't know what else to do. "We ... ah ... I guess we better get back."

Sofia smiled seductively. She reached inside my jacket and ran her long red nails along my side. "Wouldn't you like to take me for a walk? The moon is lovely tonight."

My body tingled from Sofia's touch. And my head spun. Was she propositioning me? "Um ... I ... ah ... I better get back to Maddie."

Sofia pouted. "Alright," she finally said, sounding disappointed, but not angry. Then she took my arm and let me lead her back to our spouses.

Later that night, I fucked my wife like I hadn't fucked her in years. As soon as we got home, I threw Maddie onto the sofa, pushing her dress up around her waist while simultaneously pulling my cock out of my pants. I pulled her pantyhose and panties down her legs, not bothering to take them off completely, and then rammed my rock-hard cock into her pussy. It didn't take me long to cum. I would've felt guilty except Maddie came just as fast, which surprised me.

We went to our bedroom and made love again. Again, this surprised me. To be honest, our sex life hadn't been good for a while. We've been together for 8 years, married for 5, and like most married couples our sex life waned after a few years. Nowadays we might do it once a week, but often only as the culmination of watching a porn movie on the TV. So, doing it twice in less than an hour really surprised me.

I knew what got me so hot. It was Sofia. But Maddie's sudden passion surprised me. It didn't take long before I understood why.

After our lovemaking, we spooned in bed. Maddie was so quiet I assumed she had fallen asleep.

"I need to tell you something," she finally said, trepidation in her voice.

"What?"

Maddie turned to face me, looking nervous. "Tonight ... while you were dancing with Sofia. Victor made a pass at me."

I almost jumped off the bed. "What?! What did he do?"

Maddie hesitated, then finally said, "After you left with Sofia, he asked me to dance. I must've been a little drunk, because I didn't notice as he led me into a side room." Maddie described how Victor had kissed and fondled her. He groped her tits and reached under her dress.

"How far did he go?" I asked angrily, picturing Victor's black hand between my wife's legs.

"He ... he cupped me," Maddie said.

"But then I pushed him away," she quickly added. "And I ran out of the room."

Anger flared inside me. How dare Victor take advantage of my wife!

But then something Maddie said struck me. "What do you mean, *then* you pushed him away?" I said accusingly. "You weren't fighting before that? You let him touch you?"

"Adam, no," Maddie pleaded, gripping my arm. "It wasn't like that at all. I guess I was drunk. It took me a minute to realize what was happening. As soon as I did, I pushed him away and ran from the room."

I let it go, not challenging Maddie further. But I wondered if she was holding back and not telling me the full truth. Victor had aroused her. That's why she had been so horny tonight. I felt jealous, and mad. I considered telling Maddie about Sofia, but something held me back. I spooned Maddie again, and with the assurance of my arm around her, she quickly fell asleep. But I laid awake late into the night, thinking of Sofia.

THANKS FOR CHECKING out Desiring Another Man's Wife! This novella is part of the collection, Losing My Wife To Another Man: Three Interracial Cuckold Novellas (Flash of Stocking Collection Book 3), which is available wherever e-Books are sold.

BONUS SNEAK PEEK – TINY DANCER

Sarah was dozing in the front seat, sleepy after the long game. Gina was next to her, and in the back were 4 other girls from their high school cheer squad. They were driving home from an away game, and the steady rumbling of the wheels on the road after the long football game had them all sleeping.

Gina's dad was driving, and Sarah was wedged in between Gina and her father (Mr. Moretti). The pickup wasn't small, but Mr. Moretti was a big man, and he took up a lot of the front bench seat. Gina was asleep with her head against the door window, her mouth half open as she slept. Sarah was half asleep, leaning forward against the seat belt.

Suddenly Sarah felt Mr. Moretti's hand on her thigh, below her skirt. She was instantly wide awake, and her eyes went wide. She assumed it was an accident because they were sitting so close together. Sarah slid closer to Gina, away from her father. But Mr. Moretti kept his hand on her leg. In fact, he clamped down on her thigh, preventing her from sliding over.

A lot of thoughts ran through Sarah's head at the same time. First, how freaky it was for Mr. Moretti to touch her. Second, how big Mr. Moretti's hand was. It felt like he could wrap his fingers around her whole thigh. Third, how big a commotion it would be if she screamed. After all, Mr. Moretti's was Gina's dad, and Gina was her best friend.

And maybe it was all an accident. Maybe Mr. Moretti was in a driving zone and didn't realize his hand was on her thigh.

But then Mr. Moretti began caressing her, and Sarah knew it was no accident. She stopped breathing as she felt his big hand rub her thigh. Mr. Moretti was in construction and his big hands were calloused. In the quiet of the (mostly) sleeping car, Sarah could hear his calloused fingertips scrape against the nylon of the nude tights she wore under her short cheerleading skirt. He had big worker's hands, scarred from physical labor, with thick fingers and knobby knuckles.

Mr. Moretti gripped Sarah's thigh with his big hand and pulled, forcing her legs to open. Sarah tried to resist but he was much bigger and stronger. With her legs parted, he moved his hand up her leg until his big fingers went under her short, pleated cheer skirt.

Sarah's head was spinning. She didn't know what to do. She wasn't a virgin. At 18 she was barely legal, but she didn't consider herself to be innocent. But this was Gina's dad! He must be what, 50? Ancient! And he was touching her!

Sarah felt Mr. Moretti's hand move up her leg, moving her skirt with it. She felt his fingertips touch her bottoms, what she and the other cheerleaders called bloomers or spankies.

She couldn't believe this was happening! She felt powerless.

In the darkness she heard Mr. Moretti breathing hard. Then she felt his finger rub up and down across her sex, over the bottoms.

"Please don't," Sarah desperately whispered into the darkness. She grabbed his wrist with both hands, but he was too strong. He rubbed harder into her cleft, forming a camel toe in the bottoms.

"Stop," she whispered in a pleading voice, and she dug her nails into his wrist, but still he wouldn't stop.

Gina stirred next to her. She was waking up. Mr. Moretti quickly pulled his hand back, and Sarah immediately closed her legs and pulled her skirt down. Just like that, it was over. But she was breathing hard. And she heard Mr. Moretti breathing hard too, in the darkness.

Mr. Moretti didn't say anything to her when he dropped her off. Sarah looked at him. He didn't look guilty, or sorry. He smiled at her, and it creeped her out. It sent a chill down her spine.

Everyone was asleep when Sarah entered her house. She went into her bedroom and flopped onto her bed. She kicked off her saddle shoes and looked up at the ceiling. She was still dazed from what happened in the car. She wasn't breathing hard anymore, but it felt like her heart was still pounding.

She could still feel Mr. Moretti's hand on her. Under her skirt. On her bottoms. Rubbing her.

Sarah didn't know why. She couldn't explain it. But she felt hot between her legs. Like there was an ache there.

Sarah pulled up her skirt and reached into her bottoms and tights. She gasped as her fingertips touched her pussy. She was moist. She closed her eyes and rubbed herself.

Sarah thought about the car, Mr. Moretti's hand on her, as she rubbed circles over her clit. She was breathing hard, panting. With her other hand, she unbuttoned her blouse and pulled her bra up, exposing her tits. Sarah had small breasts, little A cups. Her nipples were hard, like erasers. She squeezed them with her thumb and forefinger as she rubbed her clit. She thought about Mr. Moretti touching her. Forcing her legs open. Rubbing her sex.

Suddenly Sarah groaned and arched her back, cumming on her fingers. It was a powerful orgasm and she had to bite her lip to keep from moaning too loud. Afterwards, she was breathing hard. She squeezed her legs together and looked up at the ceiling again, wondering what had just happened.

———◉———

TWO WEEKS LATER

———◉———

SARAH WALKED WITH SOME of her friends to the Tropical Café. It just opened up and its smoothie's were the new thing in their small town, at least in her high school.

A new office building was going up across the street and Mr. Moretti was there, taking a break with some of his crew. Sarah didn't look but she felt his eyes on her. It freaked her out after the other night. That was a couple weeks ago, and she'd avoided going over to Gina's since, not wanting to see her father. Still, she felt her heart beating faster knowing he was looking at her.

"So, can we lust after them now?" Mario said as they watched the high school girls walk by. Moretti was a foreman of one of the masonry teams. Mario was on his team and was Italian, just like him. He only hired Italians. They hauled concrete and laid brick and stone for a living. It was hard physical labor and you could tell that by their massive chests and arms.

Moretti was looking at Sarah Summers. At her drop-dead gorgeous face, at her lithe figure, her long shapely legs. He remembered the feel of her thigh. Tight and toned. And reaching under her skirt. Touching her pussy. She'd been hot there. "What?" he said distractedly to Mario.

"Are they old enough we can lust after them now?" Mario said again with a toothy grin.

Moretti grunted. Some of the other men laughed.

"That Sarah Summers," Mario said, looking at her. "All legs and blonde hair, that one."

There were more laughs. The men were mostly looking at Sarah. All the girls were pretty, they were the *in-crowd* at the local high school and in the flower of their youth. But Sarah Summers was special. She was the prettiest of them, the prettiest girl in town. Everyone knew it. She turned every male head wherever she went.

It had been that way since she was barely a teen. Now she was 18, her birthday just last month.

"Shut the fuck up!" Moretti snarled. "You're talking about my daughter!"

Gina – Moretti's daughter – was among the young girls walking to the Tropical Café. But like the other men, Moretti's eyes and thoughts were on Sarah.

"Yeah, all legs and blonde hair," he thought. Just like Gaby, Sarah's mother. Thinking about Gaby made him angry. Not at Gaby, not really, but at life. *His* life. But then, Moretti was mostly an angry man.

Finally, he turned his eyes away from Sarah. "Back to work," he ordered his team. The order came out like a snarl. The men looked anxiously at their boss. He was a moody guy, and you didn't want to cross Moretti when he was angry. Everyone scurried back to their jobs.

⎯⎯●⎯⎯

"WHERE ARE YOU GOING?" Sarah asked Gina as they sipped their smoothies.

"I don't know. Carla says she needs to see someone in the city. She says me and Rosa have to go with her," Gina said. Carla was her mother. Rosa was her sister.

"Your dad's not going?" Sarah asked.

"No," Gina said with an unconcerned shrug. She was already thinking about something else, and tapping away on her phone.

Sarah thought about it all day Friday, and then all day Saturday. Mr. Moretti was all alone at home. He was going to be all alone until late Sunday, while Gina was with her mother and sister in the city.

Sarah had a date Saturday night with her boyfriend Tony. She wasn't great at math, hated the subject, but she liked numbers. She kept track of them in her head. Tony was her 5th boyfriend. She'd had sex with 3 of her boyfriends. All together she'd had sex 15 times since losing her virginity in the back seat of a car. She didn't know if that made her a slut or not. And that only counted intercourse. It didn't include blowjobs or hand jobs. Or guys jerking off and cumming on her little tits. Or her face.

She didn't like it when they came on her tits and face. Especially her face. It was messy. Especially when it got into her hair. That's why Sarah had learned it was better to swallow.

Sarah liked sex. She didn't think it made her a slut to like sex. It was hypocritical anyways. If a boy likes sex he's a hero. If a girl does, she's a slut. Sarah kept it to herself though. That she liked sex. She didn't even tell Gina.

She especially didn't tell Gina that she didn't mind swallowing. The first couple of times it had been disgusting. Then she realized the taste wasn't mad. It's not that she liked the taste of cum. She just didn't hate it.

Sarah got dressed for her date. A clingy blouse, short wool skirt, cream colored cable knit tights, black Mia flats. They were her favorite flats. She liked the shiny ones with pointy toes. She thought the shininess and pointy toes made the flats look sexy. And it was something for flats to look sexy.

Sarah brushed out her hair and put on makeup. She applied brownish red lipstick that made her lips look wet, because Tony said he liked that. But even as she was brushing on the lipstick she was thinking of Mr. Moretti.

The way he put his hand on her thigh. The way he forced her legs open. The way he pushed his hand under her skirt and rubbed her crotch. He did what he wanted, and she was helpless to stop him.

No one had ever treated her that way. Yes, sometimes boys got aggressive with her, even rough. But she always knew they knew *no* meant *no*. She always felt in control.

Not with Mr. Moretti though. It had lasted less than 10 minutes, but never during that time had she felt so helpless, or that no meant no with Mr. Moretti.

Tony called and told Sarah he would pick her up at 7. She hesitated, then told her boyfriend she wasn't feeling well and had to take a raincheck on their date. And with that answer, Sarah had made her decision.

It would change her life.

SARAH TOOK THE BUS to Gina's house. Her mom was out, and they didn't have a second car. She knocked at the door.

"This is insane," she thought to herself as she waited. Mr. Moretti probably wasn't even home. Part of her hoped he wasn't. But then the door opened and there he was.

Mr. Moretti looked her up and down. It was like he looked right through her, to her soul. "Um, ah, is Gina here?" she hesitantly asked.

Mr. Moretti grinned. It wasn't a ha-ha grin though. "You know she's not," he told her with a knowing look.

"Um ... what?" Sarah said, surprised. She'd never had anyone call her out on a lie.

Mr. Moretti moved aside, inviting Sarah in. Sarah frowned, then hesitantly stepped in. Mr. Moretti was a big man, so she had to angle her body sideways to avoid touching him as she entered. The hard soles of her pointy toe black flats clicked on the hardwood floor.

Midway in the foyer, Sarah turned and said, "So Gina's not here?"

Mr. Moretti closed the door. He turned the deadbolt. The rattle of the lock sent a shiver down Sarah's back.

Mr. Moretti turned and looked at Sarah. He gave her another up and down look, longer this time. "All blonde hair and legs," he whispered to himself.

"What?" Sarah said, not hearing him.

"She's with her bitch mother in the city," Mr. Moretti said, anger and dismissiveness in his voice.

"Oh ...," Sarah said, looking down at her feet. It was always uncomfortable when an adult talked harshly about his spouse.

Moretti moved past Sarah on his way to the kitchen. "You want a beer?" he asked as he opened the refrigerator.

Sarah wasn't legal to drink, but she'd had alcohol before of course with her friends. Being invited to drink with an adult though was weird.

"You want one?" Moretti asked again, holding up two IPAs.

Sarah shrugged and said, "Okay."

Moretti opened both bottles and handed one to Sarah. He moved into the family room where a football game was playing on the big TV on the wall. Sarah didn't know what to do, so she followed him.

Moretti motioned to the sofa with his beer. Sarah sat as Moretti used the remote to mute the TV.

Mr. Moretti looked at the young girl sitting next to him. Sarah Summers was truly gorgeous, like a teen model or movie starlet. She had that innocence and ripeness that only naïve teenagers and young 20-somethings had.

For a while they drank their beers in silence. Finally, Moretti asked, "So why are you here Sarah?"

Sarah looked uncomfortable. And uncertain. *"Why AM I here?"* she asked herself.

"I wanted to see Gina," she said, although in her heart she knew that was a lie.

Moretti grinned at her like he had before. "I think we both know why you're here," he said knowingly.

"What? Why?" Sarah said, not understanding.

Moretti slid closer to Sarah on the sofa, getting into her personal space. He put his big hand on her thigh, just below her skirt. "You liked when I touched you here?" he asked with that leering smile again.

Sarah pushed away Moretti's hand. She tried to slide away from him, but was at the end of the sofa.

Moretti laughed at her effort to move away from him. He said, "You liked it, right? That's why you're here."

Sarah said, "No." But it was a weak response and they both knew it.

Moretti chugged down the rest of his beer and then put the bottle on the coffee table.

"You know what's happening here, don't you?" Moretti asked with the same leering grin. "You know how this is gonna end?"

Sarah didn't answer. She nervously sipped her beer.

Moretti took her beer and put it on the coffee table next to his empty bottle. Then he put his hand on Sarah's thigh again.

Sarah stared at the hand on her thigh. It was big. Big enough to almost encircle her entire slim, shapely thigh. But then, Mr. Moretti was a big man. A mountain of a man.

"You liked when I did this in the car," Moretti said as he began caressing her.

"Nooooo," Sarah said in a small, schoolgirl voice. She shivered as Moretti caressed her leg.

"Sweet Sarah Summers," Moretti said as he caressed Sarah's sensitive inner thigh with the flat of his thumb. "I can tell you like it. But you pretend you don't. That's your thing?"

⎯⎯●⎯⎯

THANKS FOR CHECKING out Tiny Dancer – Book 1! The 3-book series is available wherever e-Books are sold.

BONUS SNEAK PEEK – FAITHFUL WIFE'S FALL FROM GRACE

THIS IS AN EXCERPT *from Book 1 of Faithful Wife's Fall From Grace*

MIKE DIDN'T WANT TO go. He was tired from his trip. Meetings with partners and clients about his Sapphire project were exhausting.

Mostly though, Mike hated happy hours. They weren't his thing. He was shy and felt more comfortable in small groups, not among big crowds like happy hours. He never knew what to say and always felt awkward. Especially since it was Jen's company happy hour and he wouldn't know anyone there.

But he couldn't remember the last time Jen wanted to go to happy hour, and she wanted him to be there. So of course he was going, because he wanted to support his wife.

Mike moved through the crowd, searching for Jen. Then he saw her. He took a moment to look at his wife. As usual, she was the prettiest girl in the room. But somehow, she looked different. It wasn't just tonight. He'd noticed since getting home from his last business trip. She seemed ... bubblier, like she was walking on air. More outgoing (if that was possible, since Jen was already a people person). She seemed, well, happier.

Jen was with a group of people. Although, she was mostly talking to a dark-haired guy. He was tall, had broad shoulders and a confident swagger. As she sipped a cosmo, she beamed and chatted merrily with him.

Mike approached. Jen smiled when she saw him, squeezing his arm and giving him a quick kiss. "Fashionable late, as usual," she joked, smiling into his eyes. She was tipsy but not drunk. The server came around and Mike ordered a Highland Park scotch. Then Jen introduced Mike to her friends. The tall dark-haired man was Scott.

As was his nature, Mike was mostly quiet as the party went on around him. He listened to Jen and her friends talking. He saw immediately that Scott was the center of attention. He was charismatic and charming, and he knew how to tell good stories.

Scott told a story and everyone laughed. Jen laughed and hit him playfully on the arm. She smiled beaming at him. Scott grinned back at her. Mike frowned and he felt something stir inside him.

Mike had a moment alone with Jen. He whispered, "Who's he again?"

"I told you baby, he's Scott," Jen said.

"Yeah but, who is he?"

"He's a new partner. He's really smart and talented. Sometimes he helps me with projects," Jen said.

"What is he, your new bud?" Mike said sarcastically.

Jen's eyes went wide, and she experienced déjà vu. In the past she had a lot of guy friends, and her best guy friends she called "buds." She spent a lot of time with her buds, not as much as with Mike of course, but a lot.

There was always laughing and talking and hanging out, and a lot of flirting too. Like, when they used to go to clubs, Jen often danced with her buds as much as Mike, and there was always some touching. It never led to anything of course, but Mike always got jealous and upset and often it led to big arguments. One time a few years ago, Mike got so angry he actually stormed out of their apartment and spent a few days with his best friend Sam.

Jen was a complete mess those days he was away. She was afraid she lost Mike and she couldn't live without him. So just like that, she stopped flirting. She pretty much stopped having guy friends too, and certainly no more "buds" or dancing with other men. Now her friends were mostly girls, and the guys in her life were just casual acquaintances, except for a few like Joey and Sam, and Allie's husband RH. Jen was still as pretty and sexy as ever, but she'd turned into a plain brown vanilla wife.

Mike hadn't been jealous in years. Jen had given him no reason to be. Now though he clearly was. And Jen liked it. It was like, it showed that he cared about her. That he loved her. And she liked the way, at that moment, she had all his attention. Maybe it was the vodka clouding her good sense, but she wanted to keep him jealous.

"Scott's just someone I work with baby," Jen said kinda dismissively. "We hang sometimes ...."

"You hang?" Mike said with a frown.

"Mike it's nothing. We work together, that's all," Jen said. Then she took his arm and pulled him back into the circle of people. She made sure to stand next to Scott, and they started laughing and talking again. She sensed Mike watching them. She sensed his jealousy, that he was getting upset.

———◦———

I WENT DOWNSTAIRS. The pool was empty. The basement was quiet, completely deserted. But then I remembered. The locker room and game room were also down here.

First, I went to the locker room. Empty. I looked out the window. The bonfire had mostly gone out, just embers now. There was no one there.

Then I went to the game room. I looked inside. My eyes opened wide at what I saw. I'll never forget it. It's seared in my brain.

It was Jen and Scott. The room was illuminated by a single soft lamb but I could see everything. They were locked in an embrace, kissing. Jen's hands were on Scott's arms, her fingers digging into his biceps. Jen's shorts were unbuttoned. His hand was inside her shorts, inside her tights and panties. He was fingering her.

Somewhere along the way Jen had lost the over-sized cable knit sweater. On top she wore only a chemise. And the UGGs on her feet were gone too. She was in the black opaque tights.

I was frozen, like a statue. I was in the shadows of the hallway just outside the game room, so they didn't notice me.

I'll never forget the sounds. The soft, wet sounds of their kissing. The low throaty moans. The rustle of nylon as Scott fingered Jen inside her tights.

Then I saw something that sent a shudder down my spine. As Scott fingered her – with each thrust of his finger into her pussy – Jen's pretty feet in the black tights arched onto her tiptoes.

It was the most erotic thing I'd ever seen. My head was spinning as my fantasy was coming true in front of my eyes.

I unbuckled my pants and pushed my hand into my boxers. I wrapped my hand around my hard cock. And then, just like that, I came. I barely touched myself and I came, soiling my pants.

Then I experienced the biggest low of my life. It was like a huge wave of depression, of sadness, of loss. Here was my faithful wife in the arms of another man. He was kissing her. His hand was down her pants. And she wasn't fighting back. She was kissing him back, caressing him back.

The sense of loss was overwhelming. Jen wasn't just mine anymore. Things would never again be the same between us.

———◉———

THANKS FOR CHECKING out *Faithful Wife's Fall From Grace – Book 1! The 8-book series is available wherever e-Books are sold.*

And Book 1 is now on sale for 99 cents, if you want to give it a try!

Email me if you can't find this online sale—peteandrews1701@gmail.com

BONUS – DARRENZ'S INTERVIEW WITH PETE ANDREWS (UPDATED OCT 2024)

DarrenZ is a long-time reader and a big supporter, which I greatly appreciate. He's on Literotica and Medium and is an author himself. He contacted me and asked if I would answer a few questions, so here's my interview with **DarrenZ**.

Q: *First "xleglover", your old handle on Literotica and OurHotWives is obviously "crossed legs lover", a reference to your love of hose covered legs, correct?*

That's right. And before **xleglover**, I wrote as **Flash of Stocking**. I actually can't remember why I switched from Flash to xleglover. And now I write as Pete Andrews.

I published the short stories I wrote as Flash of Stocking in 3 short story collections.

Q: *Obviously, you are yourself a fan of the genre. You've mentioned (often within your works but also in posts) stories in the genre and authors that inspired you. Can you share some here for your fans who might be interested?*

Some of my favorites, in no particular order (with some of the books I like), are:

- KT Morrison (*Maggie, Losing His Wife*)
- Max Sebastian (*Madeleine*)

- Kirsten McCurran (*Hot Dates*)
- Arnica Butler (*Zoe*)
- Kenny Wright (*Training*)

And an honorable mention to David McManus. I hope someday he finishes his series. No, I am not David McManus.

Q: *What came first, some of your shorter stories like "Aroused by Cheating" and "Opening Pandora's Box" or what folks refer to as "Timeline Alpha", the first Mike & Jen saga that started with "He Fucked My Girl"?*

The short stories came first. I have since published those shorts in *Wife Watching Game And Other Stories*, *Wife Dates Another Man And Other Stories*, and *Losing My Wife To Another Man*. And *Opening Pandora's Box* is complete now as a 5-book series. All my books are wherever e-books are sold.

You mentioned the series that began with *He Fucked My Girl*. That was never intended to be a series. But I read David McManus's 2 books, and it was such a mindfuck, it inspired me to write the sequel to HFMG, *All In My Head*. That book was my attempt at an angsty mindfuck, where the husband is imagining things about his wife (or maybe not imagining). And then the series just kept going after that book. I plan to publish an updated version of that series eventually. And the sequel, *Anna and Peter's Story*.

Q: *Some of those shorter stories had much harsher endings for the fated couple. Do you still like them? Will we see them again in an anthology or shorter releases?*

Yes, many have dark endings. A few of the darkest are in the second Flash of Stocking collection, *Wife Dates Another Man and Other Stories*.

With a short story you have more freedom to have an unhappy or crazy ending, because as a writer I'm not as invested in the characters.

And sometimes it's fun to write crazy short stories. To explore wild things. I just published a collection of shorts, *Son's Fat Black Friend Stole My Wife & Other Stories Of Milfs Getting Bred*. Just from the title, you can tell the stories in this collection are crazy. Although one story in the book is kind of sweet, I think.

With a long series, the characters become alive, so I want the characters to have a happy ending too.

But not all my stories have happy endings. And books I read that don't have happy endings tend to stick in my head the longest. Like, KT Morrison's *Maggie* series did not end the way I was hoping. But because of that it had more of an impact on me.

Q: *What was the story inspiration for "He Fucked My Girl"?*

He Fucked My Girl was inspired by something that happened my freshman year in college. Not to me. But to people I knew. The 2 guys were roommates. One guy had sex with a girl in their dorm room while his roommate was in his bed. The roommate told me about it. So that memory eventually inspired the beginning of HFMG.

And Jen's lover in HFMG and the sequels – Ricky – is based on that guy who had sex with the girl. So, in real life, the alpha guy (Ricky) was Jen's actual lover, and the shy guy (Mike) was the one in the other bed. In real life, Mike didn't have sex with Jen. He just listened as Ricky fucked Jen twice.

By the way, the Allie in many of my stories is based on the real Jen's best friend. The real Jen (my wife) is blonde and her BFF is brunette – brown with reddish highlights (like Allie).

Q: I still re-read HFMG 4 on a frequent basis. Wedding night cuckolding is a particularly favorite fetish for me and you've written at least one other wedding night tale. What makes wedding night cuckolding so good in your opinion?

Wedding night is great because you only have **one** wedding night. It's those "it happens **only** one time" experiences that can really up the tension in a story and are fun to write.

Another one is losing your virginity. My take would be a girlfriend who gives her virginity to a man not her boyfriend. Maybe because the boyfriend is a cuckold and has denial fantasies?

Or a mean (but pretty) girl who takes a rival's virginity with a strap-on. That's kind of chilling. Or maybe that girl takes her rival's boyfriend's virginity.

That's the fun part about writing, you're limited only by your imagination. The hard part is trying to set things up so when the characters do something crazy, the reader goes away thinking, *"okay that was freako but I can kinda see why they did that."*

Q: Your "Timeline Alpha" is so elaborate and follows the couple on a lot of ups and downs in the lifestyle, not to mention all sorts of subplots. Literally when I got into it I lost sleep for most of a week reading through it. Exceptional storytelling that I could easily see translated into multiple seasons of a tv series. What was it like writing these stories and where did you get your inspiration for the various lovers and the story points?

I think of this as the *Jen and Mike series*. But your label is good too.

I've already mentioned how *He Fucked My Girl* and *All In My Head* were inspired. Then I just kept writing. When you write a series the characters become alive and it's like they're the ones talking as I type the words. At some point I thought of the title, *Life After We*. So, the plot kind of crystalized after that. Then after LAW, I realized there was more to the story, so that's when I wrote *Cheating and Rivals*.

That series has 6 books that I will eventually update and publish:

1. *He Fucked My Girl*
2. *All In My Head*
3. *Making It Work*
4. *Consequences*
5. *Life After We*
6. *Cheating and Rivals*

Q: *In several of your Mike & Jen sagas, the couple splits for periods. I thought the choice as an author to have that happen was incredibly brave and yet they always come back together. The elasticity of their relationship is kind of the cornerstone of your work. The fact that they are largely the same two people in the stories reminds me of works like Cloud Atlas or The Fountain. Are Mike and Jen fated to be together and is this type of relationship their destiny in whatever multiverse they're in?*

My wife and I are not in the lifestyle. So, I don't know how it really works. The emotions, I mean.

But I don't see how a married couple can be in the lifestyle without problems happening. Especially when part of what the husband loves about it is the angst. And when jealousy amps up the husband's desire to see his wife with the other man. Especially when it's not a one-night stand, but a regular fuck buddy where eventually feelings develop.

I read posts of people on ourhotwives who do this in real life. Of course, we never know when it's real or not. But I've noticed how many of those threads just end all of a sudden. So, I think the hotwife and cuckold lifestyles are bound to have issues between the husband and wife.

So, in my stories, I'm trying to be realistic as I see it. I try to capture the emotions that result from adding another man to a loving marriage. And sometimes those emotions might lead them to separate or even divorce.

Sometimes people email me thoughts (at *peteandrews1701@gmail.com*) and I'll share a couple here. These comments have been edited only to remove possible personal information.

⎯⎯◦⎯⎯

HERE'S AN EXCERPT FROM an email from one reader:

Your stories are tough for me to read. I'm a very emotional person, and when I read your stories, I am always rooting for love, and for Mike and Jen as a couple. Not in small part because I so identify with Mike as a cuckold. While I've never been so lucky (or cursed) to actually experience cuckolding of that nature, it is without a doubt the hottest, most powerful fantasy I can think of. When I imagine myself being cuckolded for real, I get so worked up it's hard to breathe and I feel my whole body trembling. Reading ***Faithful Wife's Fall from Grace***, I was on the verge of being sick to my stomach throughout the entire story until the end when Mike and Jen finally got back together. Them getting back together made me cry (I know I can be such a wimp sometimes).

⎯⎯◦⎯⎯

AND THEN I WAS VERY privileged to get this long email from another reader, a woman. I assume most of my readers are men, so I'm always grateful for feedback from women. This is a long email, but I thought it was worth including it all.

Mr. Andrews - I'm writing, a bit out of the blue, but in response to an interview you gave about your writing, stories, perspective on a lifestyle that I've lived for the better (well longest) part of my marriage.

My "husband" and I read your series, *Faithful Wife's Fall From Grace*, and found it to be something we could relate to. While it was that ... relatable ... it brought back many of the highs and lows we still work through.

In your interview, you made the comment that marriages like ours (like the ones you write about) must encounter issues between the husband and wife. Immediately following that comment, you wrote something akin to "Maybe I'm wrong ... if so, reach out to me..."

In our experience, you aren't wrong and I can't imagine a couple not having issues of some kind ... if there is a real bond between them.

Our story departs from Jen and Mike on several fronts, of course. Every marriage is as different as the individuals who make them are different.

Starting on a bit of a side note, we read your original stories about Jen and Mike ... at least until Jen started seeing men other than Ricky and Scott. We resonated more with *Faithful Wife's Fall From Grace* because of Scott's presence throughout. Our story centered around one primary "protagonist" as well.

Our protagonist, is someone I actually grew up with. He was my first real boyfriend and was the first man I had sex with ... and the only man I had sex with before I met and fell in love with and married my now husband. I'll refer to my protagonist as Jason.

Jason and I had similar, dysfunctional home lives. The difference between Jason and I was that we wanted different things because of our formative years ... while also (on some level) needing the same thing from one another.

I wanted stability and security in a relationship. Jason wanted the reckless abandon he grew up knowing. But we both needed what we really connected on. Sex. Or at least sex with each other.

I didn't know it at the time, because of a lack of experience, but Jason is extremely endowed. In that, Scott felt familiar. I knew Jason was big ... but not how big until I met my now husband (who is mostly average). Also, Jason loves sex ... which fuels him to be really really adept at it. He's very big and he's very skilled ... a good, but not so good combination for someone who wants to be satisfied with the man she loves.

All that to say, Jason was constantly causing issues in my dating, engaged and then married life with Stuart.

The issues that we faced?

- infidelity (on my part obviously). I just couldn't say no to Jason and Jason would never stop pursuing me. As much as he shaped me for sex with him, I was one of a few that could fully take him and love it when he's as aggressive and selfish as he wants to be. I cheated while I dated and was engaged to and married to my now "husband" (Stuart)
- Stuart and I broke up several times while dating. it was heart wrenching but as much as I promised never to do it again ... I could never keep those promises.
- Jason's abilities and my responses to him, gave Stuart insecurities he would have never had without me or Jason in his life.

- One night, Stuart heard Jason "hooking up" with a roommate of mine which confirmed some salacious rumors that were going around about Jason. (We all went to a small college). It also worked to back up some stories about me that Stuart had heard about me and Jason. Stories that didn't seem to add up to my otherwise innocent persona and cutesy appearance.
- Stuart and I truly loved each other (I think I'm capable of real love. If I am, only Stuart gets that from me). So we kept getting back together. That would give Stuart confidence when I was choosing him over Jason. But when I cheated and I confessed, it would break him down. (I don't relish that).
- After being on again, off again we realized that we couldn't or

wouldn't ever break up for good. So Stuart and I agreed that I could "date" Jason secretly. Allowing that messed with Stuart's confidence and made him question how much of a man he was.

- Eventually, he started asking questions and admitted that the whole thing actually turned him on. That gave me confidence ... like gas on a flame. The flame was attractive for both of us but it was also destructive. I started loving those discussions and they started to cement our roles, sexually. In everything else, Stuart is an alpha. In sports. In career. In demeanor. All of that made it all the more thrilling for me to "cuckold" him (we didn't know at the time that cuckolding was a real thing or that it had a name.)

- That led to Stuart wanting to be closer to my "dates" with Jason. I'm skipping a bunch here, but eventually Stuart would listen to Jason fucking me from a different room. (I don't use that word often but it's the best description of what Jason and I did)

- Jason started exerting more dominance ... which I loved ... but pushed Stuart away. It destroyed me ... but did more damage to Stuart in terms of how he viewed himself and how he viewed sex.

- I would say that that damage is what led Stuart and I back together, time and time again. I have a theory on this ... but for a man that can't experience the same kind of sexual intensity with a woman that other man can with her, cuckolding can replace that or be a surrogate for that kind of intensity. With cuckolding, he can feel those rushes and euphoric heights that he can't otherwise replicate ... and so sex was changed for Stuart. I regret that because Stuart is a good lover.

- Stuart and I eventually got engaged. We tried to focus on us but I couldn't resist. I cheated again and after a while, the guilt made me confess. We broke the engagement ... but then resumed our engagement under the old rules of don't ask / don't tell. It didn't last.

- Stuart walked in on me and Jason. For the first time, he witnessed what I had described so many times ... further entrenching him. He saw how big Jason is and how my responses looked ... not just sounded.

- After seeing it several more times, Stuart eventually broke off the engagement because of how low the whole thing made him feel about us and himself. To my own shame, I never stopped with Jason, but the break up had really messed with my self-worth. I couldn't stand the way I had hurt the one man who gave me the love and security no one had ever given me before. I didn't feel worthy of love at all ... much less his. At the same time, Stuart didn't feel worthy of my respect, or the respect of other women At least, not as a lover. Jason, was so broken by his upbringing that he didn't seem to really care. He tried to show empathy, but I don't believe he's capable.

- I know it will sound unbelievable (or maybe not if you believe your stories could be true), but eventually Stuart and I reconnected (unexpectedly) and started talking and eventually got back together. We were both resolved to start with a clean slate.

- Amazingly, it lasted through our renewed engagement and into 2 years of our marriage. We had moved about an hour away ... far enough from where Jason lived and worked (the same town we went to college in) but close enough that Stuart could maintain his growth in a company he interned at during college.

- But we were both somewhat longing for the wildness of what we had before with Jason in our life ... in my life.

- Jason had gotten married and then divorced because of his own infidelity. His wife wasn't as understanding of Jason's extracurricular sexcapades as Stuart had been of mine. She divorced him and moved away. She married again and seems happy without Jason in her life. I'm happy for her. I knew her as an acquaintance in college.
- But Jason started pursuing me again. This time I asked Stuart's permission. After lots of talk and after putting various rules in place … he agreed.
- But like Jen, I took things way too far. I had started researching alternative marriages and came across what we had been doing … cuckolding. I became an "expert" on what Stuart and I needed and tried to push every envelope. (I can explain those if you want or have any interest).
- The biggest issue was the history that Jason and I had. It made him feel like he was owed a certain amount of time with me … and his natural, dominant personality pushed him to take more and more and more of me from Stuart. I thought it was doing something for Stuart that he was now conditioned to want … but all it was doing was tearing me away from him. And him from himself. And it was making me question what I wanted. Your description of Jen feeling love for Scott is consistent with me and what I feel/felt for Jason.
- Eventually Stuart and I were completely and pervasively broken. And Jason was just Jason. We divorced and I kept up with Jason. I knew I didn't love him … but i liked the feelings he made me feel … even if they weren't real.
- After 3 years … Stuart and I reconnected. Talked. Got back together. I call him my husband … but we're not officially married. We live together as a married couple … but we're not. We don't have children … which we always wanted. We didn't think ours was a good relationship for children. Maybe

having children would have helped me to focus on family. But we didn't think it was worth the risk. I make up for my lack of children by teaching kindergarten. Stuart is successful in his business. We aren't bursting at the seams with money, but we're comfortable. We genuinely love each other ... and care for one another. But because of Jason's presence in our story ... we're not as "whole" or "complete" of a couple as we might have otherwise been. There's an unspoken regret in our relationship. We've spoken of it "out loud," but it persists in unspoken ways.

I still see Jason. We both still need his presence because of how our sex has changed because of him.

Believe it or not, that's our story and how allowing another man into our story has caused issues that we will always have to deal with.

I hope you are well and that life is happy for you and your Jen. It was almost scary how much your characters resonated with us ... all 3 of us. Somehow, it also comforted us ... maybe we're not so alone in our "issues"

Thanks for writing - Leah

***

Q: *You've written Mike & Jen through several different timelines and Jen has had a multitude of different lovers. Fans have often debated or just shared their own thoughts on who they have preferred as a lover to Jen. Who is your favorite lover for Jen that you've written and why? Who is your favorite of Jen's lovers from Mike's perspective? In retrospect, is there any one lover that you could have written more about, explored more with, but cut short for the story's sake?*

I don't know if I have a favorite really. So, since I don't really have an answer, allow me to change your question. *If this was a movie, who would play Jen?*

My first choice would be the real-life Jen, my wife. But I doubt she would go for that (LOL!).

My second choice would be a young Susan George. Her movie *All Neat In Black Stockings* even has a cuckold angle to it. And then of course there is *Straw Dogs* ....

My third choice would be Sara Suzanne Brown (*Killer Looks*), although she is too busty to be a realistic Jen.

<hr>

Q: YOU'VE DELVED INTO a lot of different aspects of the lifestyle in your stories:

wife sharing; cheating; hotwife; cuckolding; voyeurism; boyfriend; neighbors; in-laws; interracial; gangbangs; domination/submission; size queen; small penis humiliation; chastity; denial; feminization; bisexual wife; coaxed bi for husband; pregnancy risk; cuckold pregnancy; weddings/honeymoons; separations (fake or actual); stripping; prostitution; age gap; tattoos & piercings; rape fantasies. (I'm sure there are some I missed.)

Are there some that appeal to you more than others, maybe some that could be considered favorites?

Probably my favorites are cuckold, cheating, pregnancy risk, condom play, risk of losing wife, dating and humiliation. I'm trying to branch into other things, like cuckquean. I'm writing a story involving a pretty and ambitious young girl, Emma, and the stories have a cuckquean (and cuckold) angle to it.

Age gap adds tension. A couple getting involved with a man they know (like a neighbor or work colleague) adds tension. A husband getting humiliated because he's a poor lover, especially if friends find out his wife has sex with other men, is always fun to write.

Wedding rings are a favorite topic of mine. On my covers, if the wife's left hand is showing, I try to show the wedding ring (unless in the story the wife is not wearing her wedding ring).

The wife changing her appearance for her lover is fun to write, especially if permanent like a tattoo.

———◦———

Q: *Were there any sections of your stories where you struggled with where to go with it once you got them into it? Do you plot ahead or go where the story takes you?*

I don't like how *Husband's Fantasy Backfires* and *Aroused By Cheating* ended. But sometimes the characters take you places you don't expect.

I'm currently re-writing *Husband's Fantasy Backfires*. Book 1 was just released.

I think *Aroused by Cheating* will eventually be re-written and released in a short story collection.

———◦———

Q: *Tiny Dancer was a radical departure from our typical Mike & Jen in how they started out, although still meeting in college. They felt like very different versions of themselves than in the other stories. What do you think makes this series something your fans still talk about?*

So, the beginning where Sarah (Jen) is with the older man in the car is a real story. It happened to a girlfriend of my wife (the real Jen) when they were teenagers (not the Allie friend, someone else).

In *Tiny Dancer,* I took that beginning and made Sarah an erotic dancer based on an article in a local newspaper about students who make money dancing. I'll never forget a quote from one of the students. It was something like: "If you're young and pretty and have a good body, you can make good money dancing, and I need it for college."

I took that beginning, and then added Mike, who Sarah immediately friend zones. Mike is completely in love with Sarah of course.

So, the plot of TD is what happens to Mike and Sarah with that beginning. And the title is from Elton John's song. *Tiny Dancer* is now complete as a 3 book series.

———◉———

Q: *"Be Careful What You Wish For" is your latest Mike & Jen saga with a very different Mike in the beginning and a single lover for Jen. This story has been on pause for a bit and your fans desperately want a continuation. Any plans to do this?*

Yes, I will finish it. I'm working on the next book now.

By the way, Greg is real. I even used his real name (Greg). The scene in the first chapter where Mike, Jen and Greg are passing around a joint is based on an evening the 3 of us had in real life, when Jen and I were dating (we were not engaged yet) and Greg was hanging out with us in my condo. If things had happened just a little differently, I'm pretty sure the real Jen would have had sex with the real Greg.

Don't miss out!

Visit the website below and you can sign up to receive emails whenever Pete Andrews publishes a new book. There's no charge and no obligation.

https://books2read.com/r/B-A-KWSAB-YZFDF

BOOKS 2 READ

Connecting independent readers to independent writers.

Also by Pete Andrews

Be Careful What You Wish For
Be Careful What You Wish For Book 1
A Cuckold Fiancée and a Cuckquean Wife - Be Careful What You Wish For Book 2
My Girl Is Another Man's Date - Be Careful What You Wish For Book 3
My Fiancee Skin-To-Skin With Another Man - Be Careful What You Wish For Book 4
Groom Watches New Bride With Another Man - Be Careful What You Wish For Book 5
Bride With Rival On Honeymoon - Be Careful What You Wish For Book 6

Faithful Wife's Fall From Grace
Faithful Wife's Fall From Grace Book 1
Faithful Wife's Fall From Grace Book 2
Faithful Wife's Fall From Grace Book 3
Faithful Wife's Fall From Grace Book 4
Faithful Wife's Fall From Grace Book 5
Faithful Wife's Fall From Grace Book 6
Faithful Wife's Fall From Grace Book 7
Faithful Wife's Fall From Grace Book 8

Flash Of Stocking Collection
Wife Watching Game And Other Stories: Flash of Stocking
Collection 1
Wife Dates Another Man and Other Stories: Flash of Stocking
Collection 2
Losing My Wife To Another Man - Three Interracial Cuckold
Novellas: Flash of Stocking Collection 3

Girls Who Belong To Other Men
Girls Who Belong To Other Men Book 1
Girls Who Belong To Other Men Book 2

Husband's Fantasy Backfires
Husband's Fantasy Backfires - Book 1

MILFs Being Bad Collection
Son's Fat Black Friend Stole My Wife & Other Stories of MILFs
Getting Bred

Opening Pandora's Box
Opening Pandora's Box 1 - Jessie Plays For Her Husband
Opening Pandora's Box 2 - Ollie Watches His Wife With Another
Man
Opening Pandora's Box 3 - Jessie Grows Closer To Roman

Opening Pandora's Box 4 - Jessie Loses Herself In Roman
Opening Pandora's Box 5 - How Can You Do This To Me?

Tiny Dancer: A Modern Romance
Tiny Dancer: A Young Cuckold Romance Book 1
Tiny Dancer: A Modern Romance Book 2
Tiny Dancer: A Young Cuckold Romance Book 3

Standalone
Playing At Work Is Dangerous: A Reluctant Wife Story